No Guarantees

No Guarantees

STORIES

MELISSA LENTRICCHIA

William Morrow and Company, Inc. New York

Recognizing the importance of preserving what has been written, it is the policy of William Morrow and Company, Inc., and its imprints and affiliates to have the books it publishes printed on acid-free paper, and we exert our best efforts to that end.

Library of Congress Cataloging-in-Publication Data

Lentricchia, Melissa Christensen.
  No guarantees : stories / Melissa Lentricchia.
    p.   cm.
  ISBN 0-688-08562-8
  I. Title.
PS3562.E4936N6   1990
813'.54—dc20   89-48638
                                                                          CIP

Printed in the United States of America

First Edition

1 2 3 4 5 6 7 8 9 10

BOOK DESIGN BY MARIA EPES

For Frank

ACKNOWLEDGMENTS

Grateful acknowledgment goes to the editors of the following magazines where most of these stories, or versions of them, first appeared: *Antaeus,* "It Had to Be You"; *Caliban,* "No-Chickens-to-Count Blues" (under the title "Fables"); *Fiction International,* "The Golden Robe"; *The Kenyon Review,* "Some Enchanted Evening" and "Relatives" (under the title "Ensemble"); *Mid-American Review,* "Red Horse Running Through Water"; *Raritan,* "From You Know Who" and "Wandalinda"; *Sou'Wester,* "A Love Story in One Act."

CONTENTS

Let's face the music and dance.

Irving Berlin

No Guarantees

Relatives

My other distant cousins I'd run into one way or another when I was still a kid, but it wasn't until my mother's cousin Mary's remarriage to her first husband after the second one didn't pan out that me and Lucky finally met, which took us almost thirty years because I lived all my life in New York and didn't go anywhere and still don't, and he lived all his life in Chicago not going anywhere either and spending his free time trying to keep the peace between his mother and all the people who disgusted her, which was a long list that Lucky's father Aldo was usually at the top of until one day Mary decided to get married to him again and he went along with it. And not remarried plain and simple but married again here in Queens with the same type decorations in the same church as before, only this time with Lucky as the best man. The best.

The only other time he'd been to the city was when he came once with Aldo for a visit, but that was when I was still in the service, stationed down in North Carolina not too far from where Ma's mother and father moved back in the forties to get away from the winter. I heard all about the visit when I got home. The New York side of the family, they were all crazy about Lucky.

I remember him on the day of his parents' second wedding with the sleeves and the cuffs of his rented pin-striped suit a good two inches too short and this wilted yellow carnation somebody had pinned over his heart. Making my father laugh himself to tears. Catching the bouquet his mother threw like it was a baseball, then sharing the flowers with my sister Angela, fifty-fifty. Hugging his father like his father was his son. Smiling at me when we shook hands like we'd known each other forever and would keep it that way.

You didn't have to be a genius to see why my folks made him promise he'd come back for Angela's wedding that was a couple of months off, and then made him promise he'd come back again for my kid brother Vinnie's graduation the next spring—first college graduate in the family, Lucky wouldn't want to miss that, even Dad's oldest brother Gianni was going to be invited who nobody in the family had talked to since he got into the field of loan-sharking. Lucky said he wouldn't miss it for anything and Dad said too bad he couldn't stay the summer, there was plenty of room, and I said, "For Angela's wedding, or whenever, stay with me if you want, I've got a small apartment over on—" and Ma said, "Don't listen to Nick. That place of his is too dark, it's like a church in there. And he can't even cook toast. You come and stay with me."

When Lucky did come back it was about a week before Angela got married to Al Leone who used to be the manager at the restaurant where she works and her friend Arlene's cousin—now Angela's the manager and Al's the chef. We were all over at my grandmother's house for homemade ravioli when Lucky showed up and said he had to break his promise about coming out for visits because he was moving to the homeland of the New York Yankees for good, which I don't need to tell you turned our dinner into a celebration, with Lucky sitting between my father and my grandmother, who was telling him the fourteen things you can do to remove the *malocchio,* and me giving myself the idea that Lucky wanted what I wanted, that we wanted each other and we wanted dinners with the family and card-playing afterward with the men and listening to the women talk about who's sick with what and which fortune-tellers you can trust, which is not too much to want I don't think. And then we were all helping clear the table, everybody talking at once, bumping into each other, horsing around, and Lucky asked me can he stay at my place while he looks for a job and he said he'd cook the toast, and he ended up with a job in a travel agency that he couldn't decide if he loved or hated, which is how he was about a lot of things, except it turned out he wasn't that way about us and I wasn't either, so he moved in on what you call a permanent basis. We had a life.

When his side of the family got the news, the phone calls from Chicago started up and went on two–three months all hours of the night after we were home from work. Like his sister Rosemary calling to say she had a miscarriage and the cause of it was her dreaming about me and Lucky sleeping together. Or his mother Mary calling to say to whoever answered the phone, "I have no son," and then hanging up right after so you couldn't say anything back. My side was more quiet about it, but don't kid yourself—plenty of them would have got into the act if my folks didn't stop them. This cousin of mine, Mario, that I was tight with when we were kids, brought a priest over to my mother who she said was the fattest priest she ever saw and who told her she should think about getting me exorcised. Ma told me she asked Mario's priest if he ever heard of Father Gianotti who was so popular with the boys, the most popular one in the parish when she was young and maybe they should make a scholarship in his honor so no one would ever forget about him. "That priest of Mario's left right after that," she told me. "I guess he heard of Father Gianotti."

Angela was for telling off anybody who gave us trouble. So was my father, but he did it sotto voce, like at Vinnie's graduation, which the ones from Chicago didn't come for except for Aldo who was already here on some business with the Teamsters, and I heard Dad saying, face-to-face with Aldo, "They're good boys. They're family. Remember Dom." He was talking about my mother's Uncle Dominick who I never met. All I know about him is he's a can of worms the family doesn't open if they can help it because of the way he was left out in the cold to die by himself. That's all Ma would tell me about it.

Lucky was for saying nothing and making everybody laugh and just hoping they'd forget to think about the private parts of our life. Even after we were together a couple of years he was still believing that he could make everybody happy and that the ones who weren't speaking to us would start and that his mother would stop calling on the holidays to say things like, "Happy New Year from the mother you killed." Lucky'd say, "I'm not cut out for this," or he'd say, "This isn't the way it was supposed to be," which I knew what he meant because his family's always been glad they know him and he thought they would keep on being glad no matter what, so he couldn't get used to the change. Which has to do with why he left for New Mexico a few days after my father died of the heart attack we all knew was coming, so we were ready for it. What we weren't ready for was the blowup that happened at the wake. And for Lucky it was like it was all his fault. He took it all on his shoulders. You couldn't talk sense into him about it.

A different Mary from the one who's Lucky's mother got the ball rolling when she went up to Dad's coffin and shook a finger at his peaceful face laying there and said, "Angelo! How could you let those boys live in Sodom and Gomorrah and do nothing? Say nothing?" Somebody else, a man's voice, said, "Don't start, Mary! Not now!" Then another said, "Mary's right! You can't turn the other cheek and look away like Angelo done!" We can't believe they're talking about Dad like he'd done something wrong, and Angela says so. Loud. Christ. All of a sudden everybody's got something to say, loud—

"Angelo let it go on right under his nose!"
"My father's *dead*!"   "Vinnie, stay out of it!"
"You sonofabitching hypocrites!"   "He's *dead*!"
"Angela, hold your tongue!"   "What about Aldo?"
"He was never home!"   "Aldo doesn't count!"

"Who says my husband doesn't count?"   "*I* do!"
"Angelo had the most say!"   "It was up to *him*!"
"Says who?"   "Nick, get your brother outta here!"
"Where's Lucky?"   "Lucky my ass!"   "What a name!"
"Who asked you, Rosemary?"   "He's better off dead!"
"*Madonna mia!*"   "Somebody shut her up!"   "Aldo!"
"This is a goddamn wake, for Christ's sake!"
"What are *you* looking at?"   "A cheater!"
"*What?*"   "A man who cheats on his wife!"   "*Me?*"
"Who's a cheater?"   "That one!"   "Hypocrites!"
"Joseph is queer?"   "Who said that?"   "*Joseph?*"
"Who called me queer?"   "Jesus Christ!"
"Angelo shoulda had those boys arrested!"
"It's sick what they do!"   "You're all crazy!"
"You don't say it's sick to my face!"   "Oh yeah?"
"Take it easy, Ma!"   "You don't say to my face—!"
"Thank God I don't have such a son of my own!"
"You have trash for a son! You have garbage!"
"Ma!"   "At least he screws with the women!"
"What about Teresa's abortion?"   "Oh, please, *no*!"
"Shut up!"   "Like mother, like daughter!"   "*No!*"
"You vicious—!"   "Whores!"   "*Infamia!*"
"That's worse than going queer!"   "Nothing's worse!"
"He's right!"   "Leave Teresa outta this!"
"*Va fa'n cul'* the whole damn bunch of you!"
"Mary!"   "Watch your mouth!"   "Queers and whores!"
"It's disgusting!"   "Don't think about it!"
"The family's gone straight to hell!"   "Get out!"
"They're better off dead!"   "Who said that?"
"Rosemary, you say that one more time and I'll—!"

"Fuck off, Angela!"   "Fuck you, Rosemary!"
"You probably *want* to! You're probably queer too!"
"Al, get Angela outside!"   "Asshole!"   "Go!"
"Where's Teresa?"   "Who cares?"   "I'm leaving!"
"If it was my kid, I'd beat it outta him!"
"You'd beat it *in*, Mario!"   "Good riddance!"
"Nick, take Vinnie home, *now*!"   "Where's Lucky?"
"The girls are hysterical!"   "They talk filth!"
"Teresa's throwing up in the ladies room—"
"It rubs off on all of us, the whole goddamn business!"

It went on. Turns out Lucky left just as soon as they started to throw blame on my father. I got Vinnie out before he hit somebody, which wasn't too easy because he needed like crazy to make somebody take it back, anybody, the first jerk we met on the street, even though he was the one who told me and Lucky once that our family was a house of mirrors which was a good thing and a bad thing, a bad thing when you want to make them take it back because the them and the us are the same, which is what drives Vinnie crazy. It took us close to an hour to walk from the Knights of Columbus lodge where the wake was back to me and Lucky's apartment, but when we got there Lucky was still wearing his good clothes, sitting at the kitchen table with some light from the window on his hands, looking like an old Sicilian widower at church, and I could see right off that he'd already gone through one cigar box full of family pictures and was getting ready to go through another one—it's a kind of binge he used to go on sometimes:

Vinnie went into the bedroom and closed the door, but we could hear him crying while we talked.

"They tried to put a stain on his soul because of us,"
Lucky said to me, and our hands went for each other like
they knew what was coming.

"He doesn't stain that easy. You know that."

"I can't take this the way you can."

"Yes you can."

But he looked at me eye-to-eye and it was like I was the
distant cousin and he was the son of my father and the loss
was too much for him, there was no way to talk around it.

"There's the others. Vinnie, Ma," I said to him. "It's worth
it."

"I've gotta go away for a while. Not for long. Nick, you
understand."

"If he was alive—"

"He's dead."

"So some of them are going to dish it out? So what? There
it is. But we have a *life*—"

"I've gotta get away for a while. Alone."

"Remember Dom," I said to him as if I knew what the
story was. I couldn't say anything after that. Neither could
Lucky.

Nick, you understand.

You know how it is when you say one thing and somebody turns it into something else, or when you think you're
doing one thing but you end up more surprised than anybody, and then you have to remind yourself that you can't
control things except maybe things like the locks on the

doors and even those you can't be too sure of—people forget their keys, they don't do what you think they're gonna do, which is what I'm reminding myself because of what happened.

It has to do with this ad I saw in a paper called *The New York Review of Books* that Vinnie brought over to Ma's when him and me were having dinner there a couple of months ago. It was the same night Ma started to get on me.

"I'm fine the way it is," I tell her.

"If you're fine," she says, "I'm the Blessed Virgin Mary."

"Vinnie, tell Ma how fine I am."

"You tell her," he says.

"It's not easy to meet people," I say.

"It's not easy for you because you sit in that apartment like a head of lettuce in a box," she tells me. Then she says, "Vinnie, bring me that picture from the mantel, the one with you and Nick and your father, the one Lucky took."

"I don't want to see the picture again, Ma, really—" I say.

I see it anyway. The three of us, New Year's Eve, dressed to the hilt, standing in the lobby at the Lincoln Center, the only time any of us went there, thanks to Angela and Al who got us tickets to see this opera called *Il Trovatore*. Vinnie and me with no hats, with fresh haircuts you could tell a mile away, him in gray pants, gray jacket, gray shirt, silver tie, gray shoes, gray socks, me in a tan version of the same getup. Dad in his black suit, made in Italy, snow-white scarf at his neck, white gloves, white fedora with a black band, white handkerchief sticking up out of his breast pocket, showing in his eyes and in the heavy way his hands are resting on our shoulders that he knew how sick he was but could still show me and Vinnie a thing or two about getting dressed up.

Ma points to me in the picture. I look happy. "Now *this* is a suit of clothes," she says. "Put it on some night. Go out. You'll see."

"You talk to me about what I should do to find Mr. Right the same way you used to talk to Angela," I say.

"Yeah, the same way, Ma," Vinnie tells her.

"So how else should I talk?" she asks us.

I got up the next morning thinking maybe there's nothing else you can do, you put on some clothes, you go out, you make like it's over, and I was drinking my coffee and looking through that paper of Vinnie's I ended up taking home with me and then I saw the ad. A woman advertising herself in the papers, which I didn't know people really did. I mean, you think about it—writing up something about yourself, making yourself look like a good deal, counting each word because that's how you're paying for it, then waiting for answers from guys you never met in your life who must be the kind of guys who don't know anybody but themselves, so they go looking in the classifieds for a date in this day and age, nineteen and seventy-seven. It tells you something.

There were some other ads besides hers, but the one I'm talking about was the biggest one on the page, right in the middle, you couldn't miss it, must have cost her a bundle. Like she was worried that if it wasn't longer than everybody else's no one would notice and no one would answer. That I can maybe understand. What wasn't so easy to take was how somebody could get to be all the things she said she was and still be in the same boat as the guy who calls up the classifieds because he has to sell his car that he's been working on over the years until it's cherry as cherry can be and he writes down in his ad all the stuff he's done to it—new this, new that, new everything. And then days go by and maybe he finally gets an offer for a measly two hundred instead of the seven-fifty he was willing to give it away for. He needs the money. He takes the two hundred. Christ. Here's what she put in her ad—

NYC Area WF, 42, 5'6", attractive, emotionally stable, physically fit, naturally energetic, financially comfortable professional woman: respectable, classy, well-educated, unpretentious; passionate but not temperamental, strong self-esteem yet aware of my vulnerabilities, sensitive but not cloying; good sense of humor, enjoys ALL sorts of people, restaurants, music, movies, sports, theater, dance, the outdoors, the indoors, plants, PBS, books, billiards, pastries, Scrabble, art, window-shopping on Sunday mornings when the avenues are almost deserted. Seeks even-tempered, sensitive man whose qualities and interests fit with mine (knowing neither of us is perfect); unnecessary to look like a cigarette ad but should be healthy and fit; should have courage to live life as an exploration of infinite possibilities; should desire new depths of commitment and self-knowledge; should be executive (or equivalent) who is willing to plunge into life's deep joys and sadnesses with someone special. If you don't qualify but know someone who does, please pass this along. Box 20. *NYReview*

I had to ask myself, what does it mean that this woman comes along who looks like she has everything going for her including natural energy but she has to put an advertisement for herself in the classifieds? And I had to say, who knows? There are lengths I guess we all have to go to after a while.

I saw myself doing it—figuring out what to say, what words to use that wouldn't put any phony glosses on the merchandise, just coming out with it ("34, 5'11", not bad-looking, physically fit but I've got a little pot on me, steady job, union member, strong family ties, homosexual, likes movies, baseball—") and then I saw myself reading it over the phone to an old Miss Classified who turns out to be Gloria, the friend my grandmother plays Bingo with on Tuesday nights and who says to me, "Ain't it a shame your steady fellah had to go away." I say, "Yeah, it's a shame." She says, "Don't say I said so." "I won't," I tell her.

It was a length I couldn't go to. The NYC area WF could do it, but not me. And the other thing I couldn't do was throw the ad away with the rest of the paper, so I cut it out and put it in my wallet, thinking maybe I could pass it along like she asked us to do, or maybe I'd even write to her myself, just to find out if she's for real. I guess I didn't know why I was hanging onto it, not at first, but I can tell you it didn't have anything to do with me being in any so-called closets about women. That I know.

That in-the-closet stuff really gets me because when I was a kid we lived with my grandmother, my father's mother—we had the downstairs, she had the up and still does but now my mother lives across the street and my father's brother Frank lives downstairs from my grandmother with his new wife, number four. Upstairs my grandmother has this closet that's more like a room than a closet. There's wallpaper in there with rows of red flowers on it covering the walls and the shelves. This closet was where me and Vinnie and Angela would go to be by ourselves if we needed to, like for secret meetings, about whatever, sometimes about nothing. It was a place we could talk in private and nobody thought anything about it. Nobody said stay out of it or stay in it. Ma would call up, "Tell Vinnie-in-the-closet the phone's for him!" Or somebody was always hollering, "Where's Angela?" "She's in the closet!"

One time I came home from school early—maybe it was a stomachache. I think I was twelve or thirteen. My grandmother was out in the garden picking dead leaves off her tomato plants and having one of her talks with Sam, her husband who died when I was two and he was fifty-seven in an accident at the railroad yard that never got investigated. I go upstairs, thinking I'll read this book I had to get special permission to get out of the library called *Knock on Any Door* about a kid named Nick Romano, same as me, who starts out wanting to be a priest and ends up getting the chair. But no dice. There's my father, home from work somehow, and my mother, the two of them sitting on the floor of the closet like they were us, the kids, talking. Ma was wearing one of my grandmother's Easter hats tilted over to the side. The purple flowers on the brim were touching her shoulder. So I go back downstairs and make myself a meatball sandwich and read in the kitchen. When Vinnie and Angela get home, I tell them, "Ma and Dad are in the closet," and nobody's surprised.

*   *   *

At work I showed the ad to my buddy Johnny-K who's the only guy at work goes by his first name because he's got a last name from Hungary that everybody screws up. Johnny-K's the guy I've been doing deliveries with for about a year and a half, which is how a while back my brother got introduced to his sister Marie and they almost got married but it fell through.

So I show him the ad. He reads it, slow. Then he asks me, "Why'd you cut this out?"

"I don't know," I say. "What do you make of it?"

He leans in on me and says, "I heard something. You know what I heard?"

"Sure I know," I tell him. "But that's got nothing to do with—"

"I heard you were like married to a guy once. Marie told me." Johnny-K gets this look on his face that says I could have leveled with him and why didn't I.

"He's away for a while, working in New Mexico—" I start.

But he jumps in before I can finish. "Hey, you don't need to tell me nothing. Me and Mr. Buttinski are two birds of a different feather. So what's with this ad?"

"Nothing's with it. It's something, is all. Like this part: 'knowing neither of us is perfect.' "

I try to hand the ad back to him so he can take another look but he's not interested. "I saw it good enough already," he says. "This woman wants somebody who's nothing like me in most areas and nothing like you in *the* area, right?"

"Yeah," I laugh. "We don't qualify." We both laugh. "We're not even equivalent." We laugh some more, but you

could tell both of us were wondering what the hell I was
doing keeping that ad in my wallet.

So I had dinner with my sister and her husband Al about
a week after. I waited for a chance to show the ad to Angela
when it was just me and her. Al's okay—a big talker, a big
laugher, an eater, treats my sister like she was a movie star.
But I make him nervous, especially since Dad's wake when
he somehow got it into his head that I might make a pass
at him and he wouldn't even know it, like we use some kind
of secret code. Naturally I figured he'd make a crack if I
brought the ad out in front of him. So I waited for the late
news to come on. Al's a big news watcher. I said I'd give
Angela a hand in the kitchen and Al said, "Yeah, you do
that, Nickie," with this wiseacre smile on his face that
looked like he'd been saving it up all night.

Angela read the ad a couple of times, shaking her head
and saying "jeez" the way I remember her doing one time
when I was helping her and Al paint their kitchen and a
neighbor came over to tell them about another neighbor
who died before the daughter could get here from South
Dakota, or North, one of those. "She might as well lived on
the moon," the neighbor said. "Jeez," said Angela. While
she washed and I dried we had this talk—

"I don't know if this ad is funny or sad or what, Nick."

"Me either."

"What are you doing with it?"

"I'm doing nothing."

"You're keeping it. You're showing it to me."

"You're right. I don't know."

"You thinking of doing something like that?"

"No, I couldn't do it."

"If not this, what? You should do something. It's time."

"That's what Ma says."

"This woman in the ad must be kidding."

"You think so?"

"She's too much."

"Yeah."

"You know who she sounds like?"

"Who?"

"She sounds like Lucky."

"I didn't think of it—"

"The way he liked to list his accomplishments—"

"All his qualities and interests—"

"You don't think he'd pretend? Make up a game?"

"He would, maybe. But I don't think he did."

"But you wish he'd done it?"

"I'd write in. Try to arrange a meeting. So would other people."

"Wouldn't he have done it in a New Mexico paper?"

"Maybe they don't have papers in New Mexico you can do this in."

"Why don't you write to Box 20?"

"And see what the story is?"

"Why not?"

"What the hell."

"What the hell is right."

"It'll give me something to do."

But I didn't do it right away. I don't know. When I was talking to Angela it seemed like I could do it easy, but when it was just me at the kitchen table with the writing paper in front of me and the bulletin board with the postcards of doctored-up New Mexico sunsets tacked to it right across from me on the wall so I couldn't look at anything else, then I had to say to myself, I don't think you know what you're doing.

I got to thinking about how Lucky used to talk sometimes, how he'd describe himself, listing things off, all the things he had to "offer," and he'd use words like "classy" and "sensitive" and "depth of commitment" the way the WF does, only Lucky'd be fooling around, making a joke out of himself, making himself sound like this great resort he'd be trying to sell to one of his clients, and sometimes it was funny. Even though it was all about how some people didn't know what a great guy he was, sometimes we couldn't stop laughing. Other times it was like he was shooting the words out of a gun that was pointed at himself or me.

When I did get around to writing something to the NYC area WF I started out with the usual stuff, like how are you, you wrote a nice ad that really catches the eye, as for me I'm all right, could be better, being single at our age is no way to live, right? But she wasn't for me and I wasn't for her, no offense intended, which she'd understand if I explained a couple of things about myself, which is what I did next. After that I didn't know what I was going to say and I sat there waiting around for it to come to me and I ended up telling her like I was talking to myself that her advertisement put something on my chest that has to do with the one guy I thought was going to be him-and-me until we got old and died, but it's not turning out that way. I said maybe she had a similar experience in her life, her being forty some years

old, and then I told her that the stuff she listed in her ad put
back into my mind this picture of Lucky from the time him
and me went fishing with my father in the Catskills and none
of us were catching a damn thing, and Dad said, "Fishing
is sometimes you catch, sometimes you don't. No guarantees. Just surprises." No guarantees. To him, that was peace.
But Lucky, he waited about fifteen minutes for the fish to
start biting, then he reeled in his line, which I thought was
so he could maybe check on his bait, but instead of doing
that he started putting more bait on the end of his line—he
tied on five or six different lures that no trout would look at
twice, and he hooked worms onto the lures so he had about
a dozen of them stretching and wrapping themselves around
the line, and he stuck wads of Velveeta cheese on the same
hooks with the worms, and then he pushed salmon eggs
onto the cheese. You name it, if it was in the tackle box,
Lucky tied or hooked it onto the end of his line, and there
was nothing in his face to make you think he was kidding
around, nothing. And I remember saying to myself that I
wanted to forget I ever saw him do that, it wasn't a picture
I'd want to keep, which I was still saying to myself when he
dropped his line back into the water with that mess of bait
on it and Dad said, "Desperado," which made me look at
Lucky and made Lucky look at Dad and try not to break
apart and then try to smile when Dad's finger pointed to the
boat that had just gone by us and we could still make out
the name on the back. *Desperado.* For all I know Lucky's
going about things in the same way he's always done, and
here I am still not going anywhere, waiting for things to turn
out, part of me wishing he'd put an ad in the paper that I'd

answer and then we'd meet again like the first time only he wouldn't care so much what some of them said and when the others died we'd still have somebody. And I said to the WF that I guess writing to her was just something I had to do, and now maybe it was off my chest and I could forget for good that picture of Lucky acting like the fish were sure to take his bait as long as he gave them everything he had until there was nothing left.

If it was me getting that letter I'd wonder what the guy who wrote it was really up to and I didn't want to give her the wrong idea, so I said at the bottom that if she was worried I wasn't who I said or I was off-the-wall she should call my sister Angela Leone at 555-0102 for a reference. I even let it cross my mind that maybe for who knows what reason she might want to get in touch with me. Sometimes people are nuts, by which I'm talking about me, not her. I still can't believe I put that letter in an envelope and mailed it. It was like I didn't know while I was doing it that I was actually going to go through with it, but when it was over and done with, then I knew. And then I didn't want to have anything to do with it. For a week I stayed away from my apartment as much as I could. I ate out at this Hungarian place near where Johnny-K lives with his folks, which is around the corner from the old bowling alley, so I took up bowling. All week Johnny-K's grandfather who's ninety-two and who talks only Hungarian gave me bowling lessons until the place closed.

   Then it was Sunday again and the phone was ringing and
wouldn't quit, so I had to answer it. It was Angela.
"Where've you been all week?"

> ("Tell him I tried calling ten
> times.")

"I've been bowling. What time is it? Is that Ma?"
"Yeah. Al's still in Florida. With his father. I'm at Ma's."

> ("Tell him I tried calling—")

"I hear her. She tried calling. What's up?"
"You're coming over for dinner."

> ("Is he coming?")

"Ma, gimme a chance, will you?"
"Tell her I'm crazy about her."
"Nick says he loves you, Ma."

> ("He shouldn't go out so much.")

"That sounded like an order. The dinner part."
"It is. I want to introduce you to someone."

> ("He should get here early and
> help me with the dough. Tell him
> two-thirty.")

"No matchmaking, please, Ang—"
"I'm not. She's a she."

> ("Who? What she are you talking
> about?")

"Yeah, who? What's the mystery?"
"You'll see when you get here."

> ("See what?")

"You don't mean? —Not *the* she?"
"I tried to call you since Tuesday."
"You talked to her? You invited her?"

                              ("Is Nick gonna pick up Vinnie on
                              the way?")
"Ma says are you gonna pick up—"
"I heard. I'll pick him up. I should never—"
"She's okay. You'll see."
                              ("My arthritis has been bad all
                              week with this lousy weather—")
"We're not talking about you, Ma."
"I trust you, Angela. Please—"
"See you at two-thirty."
                              ("He could come to my house in-
                              stead of eat out so much like he
                              was a millionaire. Tell him he's not
                              a millionaire.")
"All right. Two-thirty."
"Bye, Nick."

The *she* turned out to be Bernedette Ayoub, who calls
herself Bernie, and she didn't turn out to be the one who put
the ad in the paper even though she was the one who read
my letter and then called up my sister, and the two of them
got to talking and found out Bernie's the niece of the Mrs.
Ayoub who was Angela's science teacher all through high
school, so Angela invited her over.

It was a woman by the name of Grace Combs, who's
Bernie's supervisor at the insurance office where she works,
who put the ad in that paper, which nobody was supposed
to know about, but when she had to go out of town for a
conference about computers she let one person in on it and
that was Bernie.

"Grace is real efficient," Bernie tells us while we're eating the dinner. "She didn't want the mail to pile up while she was gone, so she asked me to get it for her and read it and sort it out—"

"Sort it?" says Angela.

"Yeah. She left me some instructions and a checklist I'm supposed to use to separate the 'maybes,' Grace calls them, from the 'no-ways.' "

"She's efficient all right," Vinnie says. "Where'd you put Nick?"

"In my purse." Bernie smiles. She looks like my sister. "I didn't want to leave you in with the 'no-way' guys, Nick," she tells me.

"Thanks."

"She's a scorcher, that one," Ma says about Bernie, "just like your father."

"So tell me about the social work you do," Bernie says to Vinnie. And while he tells her she takes this big piece of garlic bread and makes a kind of boat out of it and then in the boat she puts two meatballs and a couple of spoonfuls of macaroni and then some extra sauce. Angela gets up and gets Ma's Polaroid and takes a picture of Bernie right when she's trying to get half that boat into her mouth, and Bernie gives Angela the finger, which is in the picture too.

"Let her eat," Ma says. "Most of them don't eat like that anymore, you have to force them. Vinnie, give your girl-friend more sauce, look at her macaroni, how dry it is—"

"Ma, for Christ's sake!" Vinnie hollers and everybody laughs.

"What's Grace Combs really like?" I ask Bernie who's smiling at Vinnie.

"She's the way she says she is in the ad."

"All of it?"

"All of it. Even the billiards." Bernie and Vinnie are smiling at each other. "She's just been unlucky, I guess," Bernie says.

Ma is looking at Bernie and nodding her head like she's agreeing with the thoughts she's having. Vinnie needs a girl like this one, I could hear her thinking. This is a nice girl, not too young, not too old, thirty-one? thirty-four? Says she felt sorry for Nick from a letter he wrote that nobody tells me what it's about. She hasn't been married yet, that's good. She doesn't have that look you get once you've been married. Vinnie almost married that sweet girl who Nick knows her brother from work, but this one is sweet too and not so skinny. Ma kept nodding her head, thinking it all through, planning the wedding.

When I got back to the apartment that night I tacked Grace Combs's advertisement to the bulletin board alongside Lucky's postcards. Then I put the letter Bernie gave back to me in one of the cigar boxes and I thought maybe if things ever worked out I might show it to Lucky sometime. If things ever worked out. And so I wrote to him like I'd been doing every couple of months to let him know how everybody is, and I told him a little about the ad, about advertising for yourself, and said that's some kind of lonely way to live, isn't it? And I told him I wrote in to Box 20 out of curiosity and in case he was ever thinking of getting a hold of me that way, for a joke, ha ha, and how Bernie turned up and how her and Vinnie looked like they'd be an item before long and maybe he could come back for a visit if Bernie and Vinnie got married—which reminded me of how on that first night Dad and Ma asked Lucky to promise to come back for visits, like he might not do it. But I didn't put that in the letter to him. And I didn't tell him what I wrote to Grace Combs. So that was pretty much it except for everybody sends you their love.

Nick, you understand. Not for long.

The day I got an answer back from him was the same day a couple of months later that we had the big party for my grandmother's ninetieth birthday and her one wish was to have everybody there, so it turned out to be the first family reunion since Dad died, which Ma and Angela kept reminding each other not to talk about in front of the relatives.

An hour or so before the party got going me and my grandmother were out on the back porch. She was sitting in her wicker chair, rocking, and watching me the way she used to do when I was old enough to play in the backyard but not old enough to have ideas about going someplace else, and she'd tell me stories about her father's goats she used to look after when she was a girl back in Sicily. She was watching me while I put up the paper lanterns that Bernie brought over, the ones Bernie's aunt had sent her from Lebanon. My grandmother said she remembered the aunt from when she was Angela's teacher, before she went back to Beirut to be with her family that was stuck over there.

"The teacher came here once to this house," she tells me. "I remember her hair."

"You got a good memory, Gramma."

"Beautiful black hair. Not like a teacher's hair. She put too much anisette in her coffee." She smiles at the memory while she strokes the lanterns she's holding in her lap. Her eyes are the same as my father's.

"Are the niece's mother and father coming today?" she asks me.

"Bernie's?"

"Bernie. The one Vinnie brought. With the eyes like a goat."

"Her parents died, Gramma. That's all I know. In this country she has a cousin who lives in San Francisco."

"San Francisco." She says the name like she's telling the children what they're having for dessert.

"Is she going to marry Vinnie, what was her name again?"

"Bernie. Bernedette Ayoub. I don't know. Maybe. They hit it off."

"Ayoub," she says. "That was the name of the teacher. She had a wristwatch like a man's. Where are they?"

"Who, Gramma?"

"Vinnie and the teacher's niece."

"Vinnie's showing her the upstairs closet. I'll get them."

"Nicolo," she says. "I have a message for you from my girlfriend Gloria."

"Your Bingo partner?"

"That one. She says to tell you there are fish in the sea. She says it is an American saying that Nick would understand."

Mia nonna.

By four-thirty the place was filled with relatives, the old ones and some new ones too, like Lucky's mother's new

husband Tony who plays piano in a bar somewhere in Chicago, which didn't keep Aldo from coming anyway, and my
cousin Mario with his new bride named Tracey who's from
Long Beach, California and who Ma said was twenty-five
years younger than Mario if she was a day, and Rosemary
was there with different colored hair and two children, twin
boys, but no husband anymore, and Teresa who nobody
remembered was such a beauty who came with a friend of
Vinnie's from the social-work office named Freddy, who
brought a cassette player and tapes of opera music that he
set up at the long table where all the food was. People were
talking and eating like there was no tomorrow and no yesterday. Some were singing along with Freddy's music. The
Mary who's Lucky's mother was singing louder than anybody—

" *'Mi chiamano Mimì'*—this stuff is delicious!"
"It's Natalie's special sausage pie. Have more."
"More chicken, more lasagna! Teresa, you got to *eat*!"
"Frankie, don't sing with your mouth full! It goes all over!"
"Teenagers, *madon*!"
"Rose, you lost some weight, or what? Try these olives."
"Al did them."
" *'Son tranquilla e lieta'*—you got any hot peppers?"
"Mary, let Mrs. Freni sing the song."
"She doesn't need you to help."
"Joseph, you need some eggplant—"
"Later, Elena—"
"Stuffed tomato?"
"He'd like to stuff a tomato, all right!"
"Aldo, watch your mouth!"

"You want some garlic bread?"

"Eat it once a day, it cures everything."

"Eat what? What do you eat once a day?"

"Garlic I'm talking about! Angela, pass me those peppers."

"The red ones?"

"What's the name of Mario's wife? You remember?"

" *'Quelle cose che han nome poesia'*—these are *hot*!"

"Would you look at those meatballs!"

"Now those are *balls*!"

"Mangia, mangia!"

"Somebody put something in Mary's mouth—"

"Yeah. So Freni can sing the song."

"Hey, Tony! Put something in your wife's mouth so—"

"*Basta!* No more of this talk! Eat!"

"Who's Vinnie's date?"

"Bernie."

"As in *Bernard*?"

"Somebody help little Joey. Ah! *Madon!* Too late."

"All down his shirt."

"Her name's Bernedette. Who needs more calzone?"

"Freddy does. Freddy, have more."

"I'm stuffed up to *here*!"

"You got enough to eat, Tracey?"

"I'm fine. This is really a neat party, Mrs. Romano."

" *'Ma quando vien lo sgelo'*—"

Vinnie came over to where I was sitting on the porch. "Nick, come and sing with me and Freddy. The next one's for guys, the duet from *Don Carlo,* come on."   "I don't know that one. Besides—"   "Besides nothing. We'll teach

you." "It's been too long, I'm out of shape." "Ex-
cuses." "Right." "You sure?" "I'm sure." "Listen,
though, okay?" "I will," I tell him, "I'll listen."

> *Dio, che nell'alma infondere*
> *amor volesti e speme . . .*

One of my aunts says to Ma, "So where's Vinnie's new
girlfriend? She's not one of those who stays in the bathroom
the whole time, is she?" "She's here somewhere. Did you
try the sausage pie?" "Why's he got his arm around that
boy he's singing with? Who's that boy?" "Freddy's Vinnie's age. He's a friend of Vinnie's." "What kind of
friend?" "Don't start," Ma says.

> *desio nel cor accendere*
> *tu dêi di libertà . . .*

Teresa is telling Angela, "The tenor, who Vinnie's singing,
that's Don Carlo, who's in love with his stepmo-
ther." "Who's the other one?" "The baritone is the
friend who tries to make everything come out okay. The two
of them are swearing to stick by each other no matter
what." "How does it come out?" "The baritone gets
murdered. Don Carlo has to become a monk, I
think." "Jeez," says Angela, "it comes out lousy."

> *Guiriamo insiem di vivere*
> *a di morire insieme . . .*

Rosemary says to me, "You hear from him, Nick?" "Sometimes. Today, in fact." "My father heard too." "Oh." "Well, is he the same?" "He used to be part of a family. He's not the same." "I mean, is he still, you know." "Is he still what?" "Do you have to be such a prick?" "Do you?"

> *Sarà l'estremo anelito*
> *sarà, sarà, un grido, un grido:*
> *Libertà! . . .*

My grandmother asks Aldo, "Where's your boy? Where's Lucky?" "He's in New Mexico." "Do you want him to live in Mexico?" "*New* Mexico." "Do you want him to?" "No, I don't want him to." "Did you ask him to come home?" "You know how the young people are these days." "How are they?" "You know." "They sing beautiful," she says.

> *Dio, che nell'alma infondere*
> *amor volesti e speme,*
> *desio nel cor accendere*
> *tu dêi di libertà . . .*

I say to Aldo, "Rosemary says you got a letter today." "Yeah." "I got one too." "So you know." "I know." "Work on an ocean liner, what kind of a life do you call that?" "He's got his reasons, I guess." "Where do you want him to be, Nick? Where? In some boat parked off the Fuggi Islands?" "I want him to be home."

Vivremo insiem, morremo insiem!

"Lucky says you're the one gave him the bright idea to advertise himself in some California newspaper and say he knows this, that, and every other goddamn thing about traveling and—"   "I never meant for him to—"   "I just don't get it."   "I don't either. I never thought I'd—"   "I'm gonna give him a call, see if he'll reconsider, give us another chance, what do you think, Nick?"   *What do you think? Please pass this along. Nick, you understand. Remember Dom.*   "What do you think, Nick?"   "I think it's too late, Aldo, I think you should call him, just in case."   "In case what?"   "In case it's not."

Grido estremo sarà:
Libertà!

   I let myself think for a minute that Aldo would call and the two of them would say the right words and then Lucky would be in his car headed for home and he'd show up wearing Ma's old black sweater like he hadn't been gone for almost two years and we'd make a meal for everybody at our place, which I know isn't the way it's going to happen. What he'll do is, he'll want more time, and who could blame him for maybe wanting to think over Aldo finally calling, for wanting to think over coming back to where not every-body's speaking to him, for maybe wishing his mother would call, which is a long shot, for choosing to stay where nobody knows him and maybe nobody cares one way or the other, who could blame him? Could I blame him?

"Aldo! Nick! Get over here!" It was Ma calling us. "Cake!" So me and Aldo go over to where she's serving big pieces of cake on the good plates and as soon as we walk up she says to us, "I called you fifty times, you *men*! You have to eat this while it's fresh or it loses *everything*!" Which anybody who has ever eaten her cake a few days later knows isn't true and that's why she's got such a smile on her face. Me and Aldo don't go into what we were talking about. We just eat. I have two pieces, which if you're wondering about the weight of each piece, I'm talking three-quarters of a pound per slice. Aldo has two pieces standing up and then one more sitting on the porch steps with his belt unbuckled. It was Ma's Sicilian *cassata*. Seven layers. Lucky's favorite.

It was six-thirty in the morning, still halfway dark, Lucky was packing his car, and him and me were acting like he's going away for two weeks at most, and out of the blue my sister Angela pulled up bringing along my mother and a box of jelly buns, so the next thing you know we were eating all the jelly buns and talking about the lousy weather and what kind of apartments they've got in New Mexico of all places. Lucky went inside to get the basil plants he wanted Angela to have. Then he was standing there empty-handed in front of Ma who looked like she got out of bed with the house on fire and he took off his Solidarity T-shirt and gave it to her and I wanted not to look at him, but Ma took off the old black cardigan she was wearing over her housedress and said to him, "What?! In the street at this hour half-naked! (Look at the hair he's got, Angela! On his back too, *madon*!) Put this sweater on, you goof." That was the last time I saw him, wearing Ma's old cardigan, her mourning sweater, saying he just needs a vacation.

It Had to Be You

As they entered the county courthouse Joan said to her husband that if it were not for this brutal murder they might have forgotten their anniversary altogether.

To which Ernest replied, "Indeed."

But Joan did not feel witty. She remembered, vaguely, the faces she had seen on the local news the night before. Faces that belonged to a section of the county she had never visited. Where they lived in trailer parks. The diminutive parents of the murdered child. The bearded, delicate defendant. Faces that could have been her face.

Ernest had called them animals. Then he had laughed and said, "Which reminds me. Our anniversary was last week." He had watched his wife's face as he added, "We'll go out tomorrow. For lunch."

Joan had stared at the television. The cameraman was showing her the back of someone's head, reddish shoulder-length hair fixed in a limp pageboy. The defendant's wife.

It was Joan who had said, "After lunch, let's go to the trial."

"An all-out celebration." Ernest liked the idea.

Joan knew that she would have to hear things, see things. The rope with which the girl had been tied to the fence.

Perhaps Joan wasn't smiling as they entered the county courthouse because Ernest *was.*

What she told herself was, I can take it.

They had lunched on smoked trout at the country club. Joan felt strong in her camel-colored cashmere and her heavy gold bracelets. One for each wrist.

So she was the one who got things going. Teased her husband, egged him on, stopped just short of saying "go for it." "It" being their attractive middle-aged waitress, a waitress their own age. Though better preserved, Joan remarked, longer *cured.* A waitress Ernest described, to amuse his wife, as a T-bone. A working man's piece. A waitress who could not disguise her interest in Joan's husband.

"It's your patch," Joan said. She wore a crooked slice of a smile on her narrow face. "She likes your patch."

Ernest had once, in college, for the first few months of his senior year, worn a patch over his left eye. In order to attract the *sensitive* women. The wound as magnet. As honey. It worked, of course. He told this to Joan after it had really happened. After his eye, the other one, had been caught and ruined with a fish hook.

Ernest did not treasure the moment when his lure had suddenly given in to his pull. When it had loosened itself from the entangling edge of the lake and had snapped back too quickly. Whipped into him without warning. But he relished the look on Joan's face when he told her the story of his college prank. He had laughed at the moral of the story.

Joan had not laughed. She considered herself a sensitive woman. Like those college women who had found his wound appealing. The imagined pain of it compelling.

Which is why Joan suspected all along that she was the responsible party. That it had been the lure she had given him. A spontaneous present, a gesture of camaraderie— extravagantly feathered and fierce, in its own special case. The kind of thing a fisherman's wife would buy. A fancy hook. "For the big one," Joan had told him.

Ernest, when he had returned to the California desert from his fisherman's dream of a trip to the Canadian lakes, his right eye gone, his sunburnt face half obscured with bandages that looked to Joan as if they had memory, had only said, "You should have seen the one that got away."

It was two months before Joan asked, "Which lure?"

"El Bularo," Ernest said. He made martinis.

Joan knew the name. Had read in the newspapers about the infamous bull, run through to the heart, buckling at the knees, going down, dead, and in his death taking one last swipe at the bowing matador. Killing the winner. El Bularo. The Joker.

" 'El Bularo' does not answer my question."

"Never mind," Ernest said to his wife. "Suspense is good."

* * *

About the waitress Ernest remarked, "She isn't very subtle, is she?"

Joan looked at her husband, at his wavy gray hair. Since the accident he had let it grow wild. Joan imagined the waitress putting her petite, pretty hands into that hair. Then putting her face in it. In Ernest's poetic hair. Magnetic. Byronic.

Joan had thoughts.

"Can't dissemble worth a damn," Ernest repeated.

"She's enchanted," Joan said. She almost smiled as if to suggest, I know whereof I speak.

"By the wicked sorcerer." Ernest lifted the dark eyebrow over his good eye. He liked this game.

And so did Joan, in a sense. Insofar as she could call the shots.

"Little does she know," Joan said. "How wicked."

"You wish." Ernest was beaming.

"Indeed." Joan held her husband's gaze. Two eyes to one. She felt like a dangerous woman. A character in a foreign film, all these years.

Ernest raised his glass. He made a toast to his wife who kept him *en garde,* kept him fit. "Happy Twenty-something," he said.

Joan touched her glass to her husband's. Champagne. A festive occasion. "Is it twenty-something? I've completely forgotten."

This would do for retort, even though it was true. Joan did not count years. She did not count on anything. She waited.

"Touché," said her husband.

Ernest felt good. Leslie, the waitress—who had let it slip that she was fifty-one, that she could bench-press seventy-five pounds, ten reps, no sweat, and that she could filet *anything* with her eyes closed—made Ernest feel good.

And so, in a different way, of course, did Joan.

Ernest had words for Joan. Joan was "classic." Joan was "expensive." Joan was "subtle." Joan was "thirsty." Joan was a "ball-breaker." Joan was "titless."

When Leslie returned again to their table she looked at Ernest. As if she knew him, Joan thought. As if they knew each other.

"How is everything?" Leslie asked.

"The trout was lovely," Joan said.

Ernest chuckled. "She means delicious."

Leslie laughed along with Ernest. "I know what she means," Leslie said.

Joan arranged her knife and fork on her empty plate.

Ernest went on. "It's a *live* thing," he said to Leslie, "a thing that's got *life* to it—*that's* lovely." He looked at the waitress with an eye that set the hook. An eye that told a story. A love story that did not end happily but was worth it.

Joan half wanted to interrupt what was going on. Everybody's focus on Leslie's "thing." She also half wanted to watch, to assist. She wondered what Leslie would say if she were to see what was hidden beneath Ernest's patch. Joan half wanted to dare Ernest to do it. To show Leslie what was there.

But instead she said, "The dead fish was delicious."

"That's more like it!" Ernest finished his champagne.

Joan believed that if she were ever to slap her husband she would do it on the left side of his face. So that he could see it coming. "Wonderful you," she told him.

Leslie winked at Joan's husband and said, "I'll get you two lovebirds some coffee."

Inside the courthouse Joan and Ernest sat a few rows back from the prosecutor's table. On the same side where the jury sat. Where the parents and friends of the murdered child sat. Two dozen people at most. Joan wondered if they wondered why she and Ernest were there.

Across the aisle Joan saw the hair of the defendant's wife. The wife's limp hair rested on beefy shoulders. The defendant's wife was large. Much larger than the defendant. There was a large man sitting next to her. A brother, perhaps. An ally. Joan could not see the wife's face.

But she saw the face of the defendant when he was escorted into the courtroom by two elderly marshals. And Joan had two thoughts. One was that the red-faced, paunchy marshals looked comically alike. A vaudeville team. The other was that the defendant looked like Jesus Christ.

Ernest had one thought.

He whispered to Joan, "They should do to him what he did to her."

"Yes," Joan said. "An eye for an eye."

Ernest grinned. He squeezed his wife's hand.

Joan whispered, "I've never been in the same room with a murderer before."

Ernest said nothing.

So Joan added, "That I know of."

It was the third day of the trial. Joan heard a man behind her say that the prosecutor would be winding things up.

Things, Joan said to herself. That you wind up. Nothing to it.

They heard the testimony of a reluctant but voluntary witness. A man Ernest described as a "derelict." The derelict was unshaven. He was on edge. He wore somebody else's suit. He swore that he had seen the suspect's car, with the girl in it, on the morning of the crimes in question.

Joan did not think about the crimes in question. She thought about "derelict." Abandoned. Forsaken. Bereft.

The defense attorney asked the derelict if it was true that he had once been jailed for attempted assault with a deadly weapon. For the attempted assault of his wife, with his skinning knife. To which the derelict replied, "It was true. Sir."

"That took guts," Ernest whispered.

Joan thought that her husband was referring to the derelict's voluntary testimony.

But Ernest added, "I wonder if he meant to scalp her." He watched his wife's face as he said this. But she did not flinch.

Joan, as far as she knew, never flinched.

They heard the testimony of a medical examiner. A thin

woman with dark brown hair. A woman Ernest described as "sexless." Who explained the procedures by which semen samples are evaluated and compared. Who identified semen samples taken from the girl's jeans and T-shirt and sweater and underpants. Who said that the girl had not been penetrated. Who said "That is correct" each time the prosecutor held a piece of evidence before her and asked if she had examined it. Who said nothing as the prosecutor handed each piece of evidence to the jury. The girl's jeans, her T-shirt, her sweater, her jacket, her pink tennis shoes, her socks, her underpants sealed in a small plastic bag. The rope with which the girl had been tied to a fence in a remote corner of a public park.

Ernest nudged his wife. "Look."

"I'm looking." Joan was looking at each numbered item that was being passed from one member of the jury to the next. From one pair of ordinary hands to the next. She was looking at their faces as they touched the evidence. The clothes the girl had worn. On her way to school. On the day she had been kidnapped, not penetrated, reclothed, strangled, tied to a fence.

Reclothed. Joan was looking at the clothes the man had put back on the girl. The medical examiner had said so. Everything off, then on. He had put her pink tennis shoes back on.

Somebody had done that.

Joan saw the whole thing. Saw herself as the victim. Not penetrated. Impervious. Saw herself as the man who looked like Jesus Christ. Putting on the clothes. Saw the defendant's wife standing beside her. Saw that she was not forsaken. The wife was helping her take care of things. Wind things up.

Ernest nudged her again. "Look at the wife."

The large man was gone. He could not take it, Joan decided. One could see the wife now, if one looked. Which Joan did not do.

She looked instead at the defendant. His face was blank as he watched the members of the jury touch the girl's clothes. As he watched them handle the rope. Joan thought, He still looks like Jesus Christ but he also looks like nothing.

Joan was not a religious person.

She did not look at the defendant's wife.

The following day, as they entered the county courthouse for the second time, Joan said to her husband, "I don't want to see her."

"I dreamt we had her over," Ernest said. "For dinner."

Joan knew what he wanted her to think. He wanted her to think "had her for dinner." She knew Ernest's dreams. She knew that he believed it was a good thing to have bad dreams, sick dreams. She knew that he believed she had problems because she tried not to dream at all.

"I'm surprised," Joan told him.

"At what?"

"That you dreamt about beefsteak. Not T-bone."

"And not cold cuts."

Joan said nothing.

"Meaning you-know-who."

Joan knew.

They moved toward the row they sat in the day before.

Joan did not take off her sunglasses.

Ernest patted his wife's ass. As if she were on his team.

Joan kept her eyes on the witnesses for the defense. Two well-groomed experts who explained inconclusively why the prosecutor's material evidence was inconclusive. Then four character witnesses who said that the defendant was a man of good character. A man who loved his wife. A man who took uncommon interest in his wife's career as a dental assistant. A man who went to church. A man who got on well with children. A man incapable of violence.

Witnesses to nothing, Joan thought. To character.

The defendant was put on the stand. His voice was meek. He sounded depressed. Not sad. Joan knew the difference between depressed and sad. She wondered if the jury knew the difference. If they would be fooled. If they would look at the defendant's face and listen to his voice and think about who shall inherit the earth.

"Look," Ernest whispered.

Joan thought, If he were totally blind this wouldn't happen. He wouldn't try to be boss. He would be incapable.

"Get it over with," said Ernest.

Joan refused. She listened to the defendant. The defendant was saying "Yes, sir" to everything his attorney asked him. Yes, sir, he never picked that girl up in his car. Yes, sir, he never did any of those things. Yes, sir, he had been married about a year. Yes, sir, he could not recall exactly how long. Yes, sir, he never killed that girl.

Yes, Joan said to herself. Sir.

Then the defendant was saying "Yes, sir" to the prosecutor. Yes, sir, he was hanging out with friends that morning. Yes, sir, he had a couple of friends. Yes, sir, he could not recall their names. Yes, sir, he would call himself a shy person. Yes, sir, he was not so shy around children.

"What an asshole," whispered Ernest.

Joan thought he might be referring to the defendant, or to the defense attorney who had put his client on the stand. Or to everyone, in general.

But she asked, "Me?"

"Who else?"

Joan did not take this bait. She did not look at the defendant's wife. She already knew what she would see. A wife who could take care of things. Who would never let things become public. Who would bury the evidence. Who would never be found out. Who could take it. Who could take "I'll get you two lovebirds some coffee." Who would never let on that she knew that she was beefy. Who would straighten her husband's tie just before his execution.

The defendant's wife, Joan thought, was a dangerous woman.

"Our guy's a devil," Ernest told her. It was a compliment aimed at the prosecutor. The prosecutor was good. He was wily. He was handsome. He was intimate.

Joan saw that he was making the defendant fall in love with him. That he was making the defendant want to tell him everything. Out of love.

But all the defendant said was, "It never happened."

*   *   *

"He didn't tell," Joan said to her husband.

"You're all alike." Ernest laughed.

Ernest was happy. He was certain his side would win. "He'll fry," he said.

As they left the courtroom Joan looked at the defendant's wife.

The defendant's wife was smiling.

"She's been at it the whole time," Ernest said.

"I know."

It was not a broad smile. It was not a fake smile. It reminded Joan of the first smile she had ever sliced into a jack-o'-lantern. A toothless smile. A sliver of a grin across a wide blank face. A secret. A cut.

Ernest told her, "It reminds me of brides."

Joan did not respond to this.

Joan was incapable of violence.

She said, "She's smiling that way because her husband gets on so well with children."

Joan was such a kidder. Ernest liked that. He liked Joan. "El Bularo," he said to his wife. Called her that, affectionately.

Wandalinda

Wandalinda had been a palm-reader for two weeks; she had been Wandalinda for only three. The name on her driver's license was Linda Miller. She was not a Gypsy by birth or by upbringing or by talent. During her two weeks as a palm-reader at the state fair in San Jose, her partner, Marva, had to do several rereadings for customers who complained about Wandalinda's interpretations. "That new one tells too many bad things," said the customers who wanted their money's worth.

Up to the day she went to the fairgrounds to reserve display cages for her prize-winning rabbits, Linda Miller knew herself as a lapsed Presbyterian ("A redundancy. It goes without saying," she later said to her Gypsy friends, and they asked her, "So why do you say it?"), a well-paid but not much gifted physical therapist, an aging member of the 4-H Club, a twenty-eight-year-old semiattractive smiler, highly unattached, resentful and accepting of the California versions of success and sex and selfhood (in that order) that could, and did, create a Linda Miller.

But shortly after she arranged for the cages, she bumped into the palm-readers, real Gypsies—and she really bumped into them, almost knocking the frail elderly one off her feet. Linda Miller apologized three times; then she apologized for apologizing so much; then she felt that some explanation was in order (some explanation was always in order)—so she tried to explain her awkwardness with strangers, especially foreign strangers, despite all those extracurricular courses in etiquette and cooking for company. Have Gypsies ever eaten pearl onions in cream sauce? And then there was this girls' club I belonged to where we made throw pillows for the poor people. . . . Linda Miller rambled on.

The old Gypsy, whose name was Alethia, took Linda Miller by the hand and squeezed the hand, as if for life, and said, "You want to go with us, so why don't you?"

"Go with you?"

"Ordinarily we would not make such an offer. But we can make an exception in your case."

"I could call myself Wandalinda," said Linda Miller.

"Whatever," said Alethia. "And you can take my place in the reading tent. Marva here will show you what to do. I need a vacation."

Wandalinda found out that Linda Miller's life was easy to dismantle. When she informed the tight-faced chief of physical therapy at the health club where she worked that she was quitting her job "without notice, without delay, and

without apology," he said to her, "That's fine, Miss Miller."
Period. When she inquired about finding another 4-H member to take over the care of her rabbits, the twelve-year-old in charge of the small animal competitions told her, "No prob'." That was all. When she called her parents and said to them, "Dad, Mother, I've decided to become a Gypsy. Don't try to talk me out of it. Don't call me back. Don't come over. I'll be in touch," her parents did not call her back or come over. When she rented a truck to move her things to the Gypsy camp, she discovered, once the truck was loaded, that it was five times bigger than she actually needed.

Wandalinda's last customer on the final day of the state fair in San Jose was a type of woman known among the Gypsies as an "easy read"—easy because it was clearly her first time, because her appearance was so predictable, and because she announced her skepticism just as soon as she stepped into Wandalinda's section of the closetlike tent. "This is all baloney, of course," the woman said. "I don't know why I'm doing it."

"It is a sign of great desire to believe," the Gypsies had told Wandalinda, "when the *gadje,* the customers, say they do not believe. Remember that. And use it. Use everything."

Wandalinda held the woman's right hand in her own left one. An easy read was just what she needed. If she weren't cut out to be a palm-reader, then what? She and the woman stared at the tracing fingers of Wandalinda's right hand, the fine ivory-colored nails, the magical rings laced with tiny bells and charms. Wandalinda began to speak as she gently traced and retraced the lines that crisscrossed the woman's palm: "You are not easily taken in by false or cruel people, you pride yourself on your intuition and discernment, as well as your willingness to try new things, of which people sometimes take advantage, yet you are strong, strong and forgiving. . . . I see here that you will live well into your eighties, eighty-seven, perhaps eighty-nine, yes, and yet you will not be enfeebled, not desperate, not alone. . . . There will be very difficult losses, and awful loneliness, but also much fulfillment and joy, this is clear. Do you see how this line branches away from this other one, joyfully?"

The woman made no response. She had apparently been advised by someone—her aunt, perhaps, whose palms Marva was reading—to remain absolutely silent and still, and to keep her eyes fixed on the hands. That way, the palm-reader's powers of divination and prophecy could really be put to the test.

But Wandalinda felt that this time the words she was speaking were the right words, the right mixture, for the woman's hand was getting warm, not the warm of insult and denial, but the warm of affirmation and trust: "You have been happy, but not as happy as you would like, you have been sad as well as happy, but there will soon be a change in your life, a dramatic change that will be difficult but rewarding, and probably very easy in the long run, maybe in the short run, too. . . . Ah! this line over here tells us that you are now in your late thirties, and that you have always been a seeker, yes, and that you will find most of what you seek in life, not everything, but there will be times when it seems that you have found everything. . . . Now we will read the left hand, the hand of our past and present." There was authority in Wandalinda's voice.

She began the reading of the left hand with a guess that the Gypsies told her would nine times out of ten prove true of non-Gypsy women between the ages of twenty-nine and forty-five who visit palm-readers at state fairs, especially in the states of California, Texas, and New York. The guess was that the woman had been married more than once. (The Gypsies could not tell Wandalinda why these women, or anyone else for that matter, pay good money—$9 per hand—for these readings. All they could tell her was, "That's the *gadje* for you. They'll buy anything.")

"Your ring tells me that you are married, it tells this to everyone, of course, and is no secret, but in the palm that I am looking at I read something else as well, yes, I read that you were married once before"—the woman's pulse affirmed this guess—"and I see that you were not happy then, no, it was a bad time for you, you liked yourself very little, you liked your first husband even less. . . . But there were pressures, weren't there? expectations, so you did something you did not want to do, marry that first husband, though you believed that you did want to do it, and you told yourself that you were acting freely. Free but not free, that is how it was for you. . . . Yes, here is the line that tells me that your first marriage ended in divorce, the line of divorce we call it, which you do not regret, no. Do you see this other tiny line right here? It tells a reader such as myself that you had no children in that first marriage"—the woman's blush swept into her fingertips as if to say, "That's right, Wandalinda! My goodness! How do you do it?''—''But now you have children, one, two, yes, and your children and the new husband are everything to you, everything, but not all. There is still something missing, something you want that you do not have or think you do not have. Perhaps this missing something is only lost, lost temporarily or permanently, it is hard to say, but I would say temporarily. And we cannot but notice these two tiny lines that look as if they wanted to be braided together, but they're not, do you see? and these unbraided lines, if you read them carefully, as I am doing, tell us that there is a part of you that is together yet separated . . . which brings us to your present husband, a good man, a wonderful man, that is clear, and the change that your right hand told us about will be welcomed by him, even though it will be a difficult change, but easy in the long or short run, and even though he is not a perfect man, no, you do not fool yourself with ideas about perfection, yet he is far more perfect than you ever hoped for. Your lives together are in fact so satisfying that it is all right with you, at this stage in your almost completely fulfilling life, that he loves you more with his mind than with his heart. On the other hand—''

''More with his heart?'' the woman interrupted.

''His mind,'' said Wandalinda.

''His mind? Are you sure?'' The woman winced. She held back tears.

Wandalinda winced too. ''Well, you see, everything balances out.''

''And it's all so much hogwash anyway, right?'' The

woman drew her hand away from Wandalinda's tracing fingers.

"If you'll let me go on, I could—" Wandalinda was thinking that perhaps she had misread some ambiguous crease, that she was certain she could find another that would ease the woman's mind. But she could see that her best reading ever was about to come to an abrupt and unfortunate end.

"No. No, thank you. I'd just as soon stop now," the woman said. "It's all right," she added irrelevantly. "My aunt, you know, she's eighty-two. I guess I get that life-line from her. Bye now."

"I was saying what came to mind," said Wandalinda, though no one heard her. The woman had left the tent. "I think it was Linda Miller I was thinking of," she went on, as if the woman had waited around for an explanation.

Wandalinda feels guilty and depressed. She imagines that she has been declared *marimé,* which in Rom, the Gypsy language, means that you're no good inside, that you put yourself before others—that you're certainly unfit for life among the Gypsies, and may even be too polluted to get along in the world of the *gadje* (though this is rare). Wandalinda sees herself alone, walking for days toward she knows not where, an outcast on the sidewalks of the suburbs of San Jose. Then she imagines that she is at the door of a ranch-style house that on the outside is not unlike the house she grew up in. She is ringing the bell, trying to ignore the neighbors who from behind their heavily curtained windows are pointing at her, assessing and interpreting her attire. What am I doing here? Why am I doing this? Wandalinda is questioning herself as the door is opened and the woman whose palm she had misread is standing there, smiling, welcoming Wandalinda into her home. Inside, the house is nothing like the house that she grew up in. The air is heavy with the smells of garlic bread and lasagna. Balalaika music is playing on the phonograph. The table is set with bright green plates. A child and an old woman are laughing uproariously together. The woman leads Wandalinda into a den where the two children and the second husband and the aunt and Alethia and Marva and someone else are talking. The someone else is Linda Miller.

Wandalinda is at first less surprised to see *her* than she is to see her Gypsy friends, who almost never enter the houses of the *gadje*. "I'm surprised to see you here," says Wandalinda to Alethia and Marva.

"We make exceptions when we have to, as you know," says Alethia. "And when the eyes of the *gadje* are not unkind."

"But why are you here?"

"To tell you an old Gypsy saying," says Alethia. "It is this: You have only one rear end, so you can ride only one horse at a time."

"What about the *marimé*?" asks Wandalinda.

"The *marimé* has been removed. The vote was last night. I came back early from my vacation to vote."

"It was decided that you need more time to pull yourself together," says Marva.

"Is that why I'm here?" asks Wandalinda.

"We don't know," Alethia tells her. "You can come back with us, or not. As you like. We're going to eat now."

Wandalinda sees herself walk over to Linda Miller. As they shake hands—not very warmly—Wandalinda tells Linda Miller, "Being a palm-reader is no piece of cake."

"So I heard," says Linda Miller. "Are we going through with this?"

"This—?"

"This Gypsy life. No security. No sit-down dinners. No shopping sprees in Baja—"

"You sound like Dad and Mother," says Wandalinda.

Linda Miller taps her foot. "Well?"

"Let me give you a reading."

"A reading?"

"Come on." Wandalinda leads Linda Miller into the first empty bedroom she comes to, sits her down on the bed, and closes the door. She picks up Linda Miller's right hand and begins to trace the lines.

"I like your rings," says Linda Miller.

"Be quiet and listen." Wandalinda stares into the hand and traces the lines and says to Linda Miller: "In your palm that I am reading I see the telltale wavy line, it is right here in the middle, and it tells us that you are you and you are not you, slim but not slim, laid back but uptight, brunette but blond, and you have told yourself for a long time, as long as you can remember, that you were content, or at least on the way to achieving some low-cost variety of contentment, yes, you have made the most of your well-mannered life in your own stubborn and acquiescent way that seems to please everyone, even yourself, but who knows? On the other hand—let me have your other hand now—yes, see here? Here is the crucial zigzagging line that cuts across all the others, which could be read to mean that your future will not be the same as your past . . . oh, there are other possible ways to interpret the zigzagging line, but I am convinced that in this instance it means that you are headed for a dramatic change, are in fact in the process of a change that will be both difficult and easy, perhaps easy at first and difficult later, or the other way around, but this change will help you to find most of what you have put off looking for, not everything, though at times it will seem as if you have found everything, like now—"

"Now?" asks Linda Miller.

"We've made up our mind."

"The Gypsy life?"

"But I can't be good at it and be thinking about you at the same time," Wandalinda tells her. "It gets into my readings. I say things I don't mean."

"How do you think *I* feel?" Linda Miller pouts.

"Free but not free," says Wandalinda. "Tough toasties."

"So what do we do now?"

"We eat."

When they join the others, Wandalinda discovers that she has been one of the topics of conversation.

"Alethia tells me you feel guilty about the reading you gave me," the woman says to Wandalinda. "What you said about my husband's heart, or was it his mind? Isn't that funny, that I almost believed it?"

"I think it was Linda Miller—"

"You don't need to explain, dear," the woman says. "No harm done."

Then Linda Miller is handing Wandalinda a hunk of garlic bread. Wandalinda breaks the hunk into two pieces and hands a piece back to Linda Miller, holding it in front of Linda Miller's mouth. Linda Miller takes a bite of the bread that Wandalinda is holding for her. Then she holds out a piece for Wandalinda. They feed each other garlic bread and laugh with their mouths full until their faces are as red as wine. Around them the children are dancing and waving their hands in the air and asking of Wandalinda, "Will you read my palms?" "Mine too?"

Wandalinda stepped out of the sticky warm tent. The woman was standing right outside in the shade of the multicolored awning.

"You're still here!" said Wandalinda.

"My aunt isn't done yet," the woman said. "She's in there, with the one called Marva."

"You forgot to pay me." Wandalinda smiled at the woman.

"Oh my! I'm sorry. I must have been—" the woman sputtered. She thought it peculiar, under the circumstances, that the palm-reader was smiling at her. She reached into her purse for her wallet.

"Don't," said Wandalinda. "There is an old Gypsy saying. It is one of the oldest sayings we Gypsies know. And it is this: No reading can be true unless silver changes hands."

"You mean the reading you gave me is—?"

"Not true. Null and void."

"Not true," repeated the woman.

"Would you like me to do it over?" asked Wandalinda.

"No, really, I'd rather not. But I didn't mean to walk out without paying. I—"

"You don't need to explain," said Wandalinda as if she'd been a Gypsy all her life. "See you around." She turned and headed for the nearest snack bar. Her vision had made her hungry.

"Thanks anyway, Miss Linda!" the woman called out after her.

"It's Wandalinda!" Wandalinda called back.

"Whatever," said the woman.

No-Chickens-to-Count Blues

An anti-fable

There was once a child and a woman and a shack in a land that was either so wet that the walls of the shack turned to mushroom or so dry that the woman turned to brittle brown leaf and disappeared if the child forgot to press the fragile leaf within the pages of his book until the rains came and made the woman soggy again and sullen.

One time when the dry wind was so fierce and electric that the child was fearful the shack would die, he forgot the brittle woman and she crumbled and was blown into the dusty corners of the shack. After days and days the child finally found her, scattered and much older than he remembered. It took the child many months in the crackling heat to fit the woman's withered pieces back together and glue them with what little spit he had. And after that he never again forgot to hide the woman within the pages of his book when the dryness swept over the land and made nettles of her despair.

There was nothing for the child to do when the land was dead from thirst but sit upon his book and eat the ants and wait inside the shack whose papery walls did their best to protect him from the hot relentless wind. There was nothing for the child to do when the land was soaked and drowning but open the book and wear it upon his head (to quiet the constant noise of the rain) and wait for the sullen woman to beat her head against the shack's tin door, for when she was bruised and finished she would remember the child and play the game with him in which they imagined they were fishes swimming upstream, trying to get home, succeeding.

Rarely did the woman speak. It used to be that she spoke to the shack of her secret wish for a house made of stone and an oven that smiled when she filled it with bread and a fig tree that danced in pink afternoon light. It used to be that she spoke to the child of the lady fat from wines and cheeses who had come from the West to take color pictures of the shack and to give the woman two dozen jars of jam and to hand the child the book of fables. It used to be that the woman said, There is no color here, there is no bread, there is no reading. And the child used to stare in wonder at the woman's angry eyes and did not understand when the anger turned to sorrow and the sorrow to almost nothing.

Then one time the woman felt so wretched as she beat her sodden head against the shack's tin door that she did not see what the child saw, she did not hear what the child heard: the wet flutter of spongy birds and beasts as they fell from the woman's wounded head and landed in a heap on the shack's dirt floor; the damp voices of words as they did the same, complaining if they landed on their backs. While the woman cried and cursed the land that did not belong to her nor she to it, the child took up handfuls of the limp living figures that fell from her head and displayed them to the shack as if their prayers had been answered.

The shack had never seen the child smile, and it was such a magical sight that she straightened up and did her best to smile back as she remembered her only dream and said to herself: I dreamed that this would happen, that these ingenious figures would invade the woman while she lie leafy and helpless within the pages of the book. I dreamed that the woman would not endure their presence, would rather be empty of everything than full of wisdoms that change nothing in this homeless land. I dreamed that animate rumors would make a muddy mess of my soft dirt floor. I dreamed of the smile on the child's face. And in my dream I was afraid.

But the fabulous creatures so excited the child that he did not sense the shack's concern. He did not touch the woman's arm as he usually did when she finished beating her head against the shack's tin door. He did not see the woman capture a tiny plump chicken and try to eat it, and then spit it out as she had long ago spit out the useless jam. He did not pay attention when the woman began to play the game of the fishes swimming upstream, trying to get home, succeeding. Nor did he notice when the woman finally gave up forever and went to sleep atop the now blank pages of the book of fables.

At first the words and creatures were floppy and wet and as passive as everything else in the drowning land. But it was not long before the dryness arrived in the night and the child's pliable playthings grew restless and mobile and quick. There was so much confusion inside the shack that for days on end the child did not eat or sleep. For days on end he tried to make pets of creatures as crafty as men and laughed at their bites that he mistook for play. For hours and hours he dug holes in the shack's dirt floor for the birds and the beasts to hide in, and then filled the holes back up when they refused.

As the days went by the words and the creatures grew clamorous and rude, but the child happily mimicked their strange sounds and spread jam on the shack's dirt floor for them to eat and tried to teach them his language even though they ignored him. With bits and pieces of the shack's old walls he made miniature shacks for his new companions and thought that they would love their shacks as much as he did his own, but he was mistaken. So instead he watched and smiled as they swarmed this way and that, in large groups and small, words and beasts of all kinds, and birds too static to fly.

At first the shack said nothing when the child one day asked her, What are they doing? What game is it that they play? The shack did not want to say. But when he asked her again, What are they doing? What game is it that they play? the shack could not make herself lie to the child. They are fighting, the shack replied. And the next day when he asked her again, Now what are they doing? the shack was forced to say once more, They are fighting. And she had to watch one corner of the child's dreamy smile disappear as he asked her three times, What is wrong?

Within her wrinkled ruined walls the shack began to

weep. And then she told the child to lean against her as she spoke to him about the book of fables: The book has served you well, Child, as keeper of the brittle woman who was once your mother until this land where there are no chickens to count before they hatch convinced her she was no one. The book has served you well as bed and as chair and as hat to quiet the constant noise of the rain.

But it used to be, the shack went on, that inside the book there lived some tales that do not gladly see themselves as beds or chairs or hats. It used to be that these words and beasts that swarm confused across my soft dirt floor were fixed on separate pure-white pages. It used to be that each separate story had a separate ruler whose job it was to teach us what things mean and how to act. Be modest, be humble, be content with your lot, do not desire a house made of stone. This is what the strongest rulers spoke, and as long as their stories were separate and tidy they lived in peace within the pages of the book. Now mixed together in a one-room shack that is either too damp or too dry, they find each other appalling. Now face-to-face on my soft dirt floor, the Applications are at war, everything has changed. The woman who absorbed them has refused them, the book cannot take them back, they have no purpose here. There is nothing they can teach us, no warnings that apply in this land where there is nothing to want or to become, where there is no chance that we might attempt to taste the grapes or eat the cheese or pretend that we are peacocks. There is nothing else for them to do but turn upon themselves and fight to prove which one of them is truest, which one will last the longest in the dearth that is this land.

What should I do? the child asked. And the shack replied, You must open my frail tin door and let them out of here, all of them, soon.

I cannot let them out, the child told her. Your door can no longer be opened. Look.

Just inside the shack's tin door a flock of frightened sheep pushed dirt and debris upon a growing mound that would trap the rest inside. Beside them a wolf in sheep's clothing hurled lifeless words, dead fir trees, and half-eaten lions onto the pile. Atop the rising barricade stood a haughty Application whose victories thus far had stretched him out with words beyond his own.

Come away from there, Child, said the weeping shack. It is worse than I suspected.

I will stop them, said the child whose miraculous smile had completely disappeared. I am so much bigger.

But at that very moment the child felt a stinging in his foot. And when he sat upon the shack's dirt floor to examine his small wound, he felt a stinging in his side, in his stomach, in his back.

Stupid boy! Know thy place and keep it! said the haughty Application as he stung the child with a sharpened shepherd's staff. But the child did not understand these words, he had no place to know or keep. And then he felt a piercing in his scrawny thigh. He saw a tiny shepherd lying dead atop the barricade. He saw the stabbing of a bright red fox.

Come over to the book, the shack pleaded with the child. Lie upon the pages and go to sleep. Come quickly, the shack repeated.

And so the child curled up upon the empty pages of the

book of fables, and he was too startled to wonder where the woman went who had once been his mother. He watched the war and listened to the weeping of the shack. He listened to the deaths of turtles who once wanted to fly and now were used as weapons. He listened to the mournful screams of peddlers who had lost their purpose. He listened to the roar and hiss of useless words that had turned upon themselves. He listened to the blistering wind that flung its heat against the shack's tin door. And then the child went to sleep.

Three days later only the shack remained. And as she looked about her, she said to herself, At least the child did not have to witness the gaping holes they finally made in my parched walls. At least he did not have to see the corpses everywhere, left unburied by those who escaped. At least he did not have to hear me pray in my strongest voice for a wind so fierce and electric that it would blow me down forever. For then I, too, might lie upon the book and go to sleep and disappear within its pages where the child and the woman now abide without meaning.

Some Enchanted Evening

Even though Maggie Evans had been the secretary at Sam DiCielo's small accounting firm for seven years, she had never been to the boss's house. So she didn't mind when she was awakened early that Saturday morning and asked to come right over. She could always catch up on her beauty sleep. Besides, it was like right out of the movies to be called at a quarter to eight by a handsome-sounding detective who said he needed her to identify the bodies.

As soon as she arrived at the DiCielo house, Maggie knew that she had overdressed—but better over than under, she thought while she watched herself shaking hands with the three men who came out to meet her. With her free hand Maggie fiddled with the large heart-shaped earrings that had been a gift from the boss's wife, Muriel Fontaine. Maggie had seen her only once, outside the office. It occurred to her that Muriel had looked like somebody, but she couldn't remember who, not then, not now.

Maggie was escorted to the basement, where she told the men who wrote down almost everything she said that the two bodies were "a sight to behold." She asked, "Are these people Egyptians or something?" And she added, "I don't know any foreigners."

It was in March in New York City in 1947, during the intermission of a performance of *Brigadoon,* that Sam DiCielo, then twenty-four years old, a veteran, wearing a borrowed dark blue suit and the gray fedora he had brought back with him from the war, bumped into Muriel Fontaine and splashed his scotch and soda onto her bare neck and shoulders. What surprised him even more than her thick, braided crown of light brown hair—which Muriel had decorated with several pieces of costume jewelry—was that she allowed him to take out his handkerchief and pat dry her glistening skin.

Muriel might have seemed to the ordinary onlooker to be gazing demurely at the plush red carpet, but she was watching Sam's hand move the handkerchief over her shoulders, and she was wondering why a man with his extraordinary good looks would bite his fingernails to the quick. Sam's face took her breath away. She had never seen anything like it. He was the French, the Arabian, the Oriental, and the Italian leading man all at once. It would be weeks before she would notice that Sam was a good two inches shorter than she was, and still it couldn't have mattered less.

When Sam returned his handkerchief to its pocket, Muriel touched the scar that arched halfway down his cheek from the outer corner of his right eye. They left the theater together immediately thereafter. Muriel told Sam as they walked to the nearest café that he was the only man she had ever met who made her feel as if she were really someone else, and Sam said he knew exactly what she was talking about.

After that, for the next four nights in a row, Sam and Muriel went to see *Brigadoon.* On the fifth night, after work, Sam went to a pawn shop and hocked his medals, his shotgun, and the gold Statue of Liberty cufflinks that he'd won in a raffle on the feast day for Santa Rosalia two days before he was sent overseas. With the money, he bought a portable record player, a new recording of *Pal Joey,* a pound of provolone, two loaves of Italian bread, and a silver-plated ring inscribed with the words *From This Day On*—all of which he took over to Muriel's small apartment in the Village. In one corner of the living room/kitchen, Muriel stacked the curtains and pillowcases and other people's clothes that she took in for mending and alterations. Sam set up the record player, sliced the bread and the cheese. Muriel opened one of those bottles of Chianti that sits in its own basket. Sam turned up the music. The next day they were married.

The older detective, who kept his glasses on a chain around his neck, offered Maggie a cigarette. She accepted it without looking into his face. Maggie had pinned her wavy red hair too hastily into a bun at the nape of her neck, and it was already starting to unravel. She tucked discreetly at her hair and said, "All I know about Sam's personal life is that he really keeps to himself, him and his wife." Maggie looked around for an ashtray. She didn't want to flick her ashes just anywhere, the way the older detective was doing. "I mean, I invited them once, you know, for drinks and chips. But they couldn't make it." She moved as far away from the bodies as she could so that the ashes from her cigarette wouldn't land on them. "I guess Sam and Muriel are real squares," Maggie said.

Ten years before the night in question, Muriel and Sam got, as they put it, their "chance of a lifetime." So Sam cashed in his savings bonds and his shares in Beck & Beck Accountants, where he had worked since he'd returned from the war; then he arranged to open a small office of his own upstate, which the younger of the Becks referred to as "Nowheresville." When Sam made his farewells to his co-workers and his clients, he told them, "We're going over the rainbow, the ship has come in for me and Muriel, there's no business like show business." Muriel wrote notes to the well-to-do homemakers for whom she had worked as a seamstress all those years. She informed them that she was closing up shop, that everything was coming up roses, this time for her. While they waited for the moving van to arrive, Sam and Muriel reread for the hundredth time the papers concerning the property that Muriel had just inherited from her paternal grandmother, Eliza, the only person in her family who never questioned in the slightest Muriel's need, at age eleven, to change her last name from Brown to Fontaine, for good.

Sam and Muriel had been handed the papers and the keys to their chance of a lifetime by a hot, heavyset young lawyer who picked at his teeth with a metal fingernail file, stared openly at Sam's crotch, and said, "Guess it was time that old lady aspired." Within thirty-six hours they were driving north, the moving van close behind them, to the ten-acre farm that Eliza had "procured"—that was the word she had used—in the summer of 1917, and had managed, despite the rumors, despite the battles among the children of her second and third husbands, and despite the intermittent raids carried out by humorless government agents in search of pacifists, to hang onto for forty years and bequeath precisely as she wished.

During the long drive that took them farther and farther away from the city, Sam and Muriel did not speak. They longed for the space and the isolation of the upstate farm far too much to say so. In their nervous silence they tried to convince themselves that there would be no mistake, no hitch, no one who would come around and ruin their plans. It was almost sunset when they finally arrived. Sam was near trembling when he parked the car on the dirt road in front of the old farmhouse. Muriel did not take her eyes off him as he got out of the car and stood for a long time like an orchestra conductor, with his hands lifted and opened out toward the pines and the birches and the green meadows portioned out by quaint log fences. Finally he turned to Muriel and said, "We'll call the place Bali Ha'i."

*   *   *

Maggie managed to straighten the exotic clothes that the corpses were wearing without unclasping their hands. She said out loud that anyone who would go to all this trouble shouldn't be left "mussed up." She thought that maybe the two detectives and the coroner had run out of questions to ask her because they were watching her without saying a word. So she said, "Muriel kept the phone off the hook for the last five days. That's really strange, don't you think? Did you see *Dial M for Murder*?"

The day after they moved in, Muriel drew up some plans and Sam hired some carpenters who knocked out walls and made small rooms disappear, so that the old farmhouse was soon reminiscent of a gym or a concert hall. At one end of this prodigious space they built a wall of windows, floor to ceiling, over thirty feet high, that faced the woods. "Wild mushrooms grow in those woods," Sam told the workmen. Then, above the center of this grand room, the carpenters constructed a cathedral ceiling that could be opened at the touch of a button. "Just push this thing here," one of the carpenters explained. Sam and Muriel had never seen anything like it before in real life. Once it was installed, they did not know how they had survived without it. "Real moonlight makes all the difference," Muriel said to the carpenters as they finished their work in the main part of the house and prepared to reorganize the kitchen, the bedroom, the dressing room and bath which, according to the plans, were all to be located at the remotest end of the house, out of sight and out of mind. The rest of the space, which after the reconstruction comprised some 4800 square feet—including the eerie fantastic basement whose antiquated walls were made of thousands of blue-gray stones—became Sam and Muriel's stage.

Maggie's last question was directed at the younger detective, whose voice didn't turn out to be the handsome-sounding one she had spoken to on the phone. The handsome voice belonged to the older detective. But the younger one made up for it, in Maggie's estimation, by looking "at least a little bit" like Troy Donahue. Before he could respond to her, Maggie went on to say that she was absolutely certain about Muriel taking the phone off the hook because Sam always eats his lunch at Iva's Dinette across the street from his office. "I mean *always*," Maggie said. "Then this week he starts going home for lunch. Right out of the blue. Completely."

Muriel might have been surprised to learn that Sam's secretary knew about the phone being off the hook. Under different circumstances, Maggie's apparent interest in their affairs might even have intrigued, though not concerned, the boss's wife. But during the week in question, Muriel was more preoccupied than usual. How much or how little Maggie knew did not and could not matter. Muriel's attention was focused on the upcoming performance. She had somehow, quite untypically, fallen behind schedule. There was still so much to do. She could barely keep up. Certainly she could waste no time on the telephone trying to be civil to the strangers who wanted to sell her things she had no use for—subscriptions to *Life,* bomb shelters. And she could not let her concentration be disturbed by the former customer who, every year since Muriel had left the city, began calling around the holidays to complain that her Christmas decorations were again going to be a "total disaster" because Muriel would not agree to "pick up her goddamn needle and thread" and, as the lady phrased it, "put out."

When Sam came home for lunch to give her a hand on the second of the last five days, Muriel was out in the barn painting some props. "Something's coming," she told him. "I don't know what it is. The air is humming."

"He said he had to go home to talk to Muriel," Maggie explained as she accepted another cigarette from the older detective who, with his glasses on, looked to Maggie like a short, plump version of President Johnson. "When I asked him, 'Why don't you just call her?' all he does is give me this funny look. Like him and Muriel were doing who-knows-what for lunch." Maggie laughed nervously and put her hand over her mouth. She pushed the sleeves of her green angora sweater up to her elbows and then pulled them back down to her wrists. The younger detective asked if she could tell them more precisely what kind of look Sam had given her. Maggie said she thought she could imitate it "right on the nose," all she needed was a mirror. "A big one, please," she said.

Muriel Fontaine and Sam DiCielo saw no reason to tell Maggie Evans or anyone else, for that matter, that they had been performing, just the two of them, sans audience, sans anyone, for twenty years—since that night they had done *Pal Joey* together in Muriel's apartment in the Village. Prior to their move to the cavernous farmhouse, they had first lived in a three-room apartment that they had kept virtually unfurnished in order to leave space for the dance numbers. Later, after Sam became a partner at Beck & Beck, he and Muriel had transformed an old two-bedroom brownstone into an almost adequate theater.

The neighbors had complained. They had asked Sam to "do something" about the strangers who were always coming and going at Sam and Muriel's house late at night. "We've seen a colored man and woman, that's right, leave your place about eleven-thirty, that's P.M., and then *go back in* after midnight," the neighbors said. "And another time we saw something—couldn't tell if it was a man or a woman or what—dressed all in green like some darn fairy. It went out late and went back in late. We don't like it," they said. "Not to mention the noise."

But Sam and Muriel liked nothing better than a starlit stroll after an evening performance. It never occurred to them to change into their street clothes. Nor did they understand why the neighbors failed to recognize Porgy and Bess and the others. It came down, they agreed, to a question of artistic integrity. "Let them stop and stare," said Sam. "They don't bother me."

Muriel's forte in all of this was jazz ballet, though she also had an excellent soprano range. Sam choreographed the tap routines and designed most of the sets. And he was the one, there was no doubt about it, with the special voice. Muriel once wrote a review of Sam's vocal gifts under the pseudonym M. F. LaBelle—a review that only she and Sam would read, of course—in which she pointed out that he could sing the heavy baritone roles "with very unusual sweetness and grace" as well as some tenor parts, if the tessitura were not too high, "with thrilling sensual power indeed."

Their repertoire up to that Friday in December of 1967 consisted exclusively of American musicals, and primarily of those musicals that were not predictably, monotonously up-beat, like *Carousel* and *Porgy and Bess* and *The King and I* and *West Side Story*. To Sam and Muriel it was natural, inevitable even, especially after Sam's better-than-Pinza performance in their last run of *South Pacific,* that they should now be ready, in their prime of life, to take on one of the grand works of Mister Giuseppe Verdi.

Maggie sat in the canvas director's chair that the younger, blond detective had carried down to the basement for her along with the large hand mirror that she used to demon-strate Sam's "look." She watched the men write things down in their palm-size notepads as she chatted about her boss. "He's the shy type," she said, "but sweet, you know, like Perry Como or somebody." Maggie knew nothing of Sam's life as a leading man, but she reported that when he returned to work after lunch on Friday "he was really like in some other world." Maggie noticed that the coroner's Hawaiian shirt didn't quite hide his stomach and that the blond detective watched her legs each time she recrossed them. "I had no idea," Maggie continued, "that Sam would live in a house like this. I mean, with that big statue in the living room and all."

On Friday, Sam and Muriel had tomato soup and saltines for lunch. Sam remarked that it was one of those December days when the very air smells like old songs. Muriel said she felt younger than springtime. After lunch, they went over the arrangements they had made regarding the lighting effects that Sam would regulate throughout the performance with a remote-control device. Then they tested the stereo system that would later supply them with full orchestral accompaniment and all but the two principal singers, whose roles would be filled in by Sam DiCielo and Muriel Fontaine.

"Remember our luckiest break?" asked Sam as he cleaned the records with a special cloth. "How could I forget!" said Muriel. The "luckiest break" they referred to came about when an acquaintance from the business school at Columbia told them about the Everything-But Recording Company, which offers its clients made-to-order recordings with whatever deletions or excisions are requested. The idea is that the customer would then be able to substitute for the missing part. The acquaintance was a so-so pianist who had custom-made recordings of every record Glenn Gould had made up to the point, minus, of course, Glenn Gould.

Before he returned to his office, Sam helped Muriel drag the sphinx from the barn into the house. Altogether it was about thirty feet high, but its head was detachable. Even so, they had to take the large front doors off the hinges in order to get the thing inside. But once it was set in place, center stage, beneath the open cathedral ceiling, it no longer resembled a thing that mortals could maneuver. It looked nothing like a papier-mâché sphinx. It had become a sphinx carved from a mountain of lapis lazuli, as immovable as midnight. "It's real," said Muriel, resting her hand on one of the huge front paws, between which was an electronically controlled trapdoor, a secret entrance to the basement below.

When pressed for more details, Maggie recalled that at around 4:45 on Friday, as Sam was getting ready to leave for the day, he was "definitely" talking to himself. "I wasn't trying to hear what he was saying, but I was pretty sure I heard the word *pinochle*—that's a card game, like bridge, sort of." The older detective nodded and wrote the word *pinochle* in his notepad. The coroner looked over the older detective's shoulder to see how he had spelled it. The

younger detective smiled at Maggie and forgot to write anything down. "Anyway," Maggie said, "I asked him if he was
going out to play some pinochle and have some fun for a
change." She recrossed her legs and smoothed her white
wool skirt. "He just put on that gray hat he wears to work
every day and said to me, 'Pinnacle, Mag, pinnacle.' Whatever game *that* is!"

By five o'clock Friday afternoon, Muriel had finished ar-
ranging her hair and doing her makeup. Her hair had been
light brown that morning. Now it was almost black except
for the stunning auburn highlights she had streaked into the
tips of her waist-length curls. She stared at herself in the
mirror that was framed with a hundred tiny light bulbs.
"Yes," she said.

She was sitting at the long dressing table whose original
spot, according to the owner of the flea market in Remsen,
had been backstage at Ziegfeld's theater. "I should always
have had hair this color," Muriel said to her reflection. "And
these eyes." She had been especially daring with her
makeup, but meticulously careful about hiding the extravagance. A novice in the techniques of self-transformation
would never be able to detect the artifice, never be able to
tell that the dark brown eyes that stared into the mirror, fully
transcendent and just as fully sensuous, were no longer the
eyes of Muriel Fontaine.

She was grateful beyond measure that she had not been
born with the kind of beauty that can overpower makeup

and costumes. "I would rather become a beautiful woman than be one," she had once said to her husband. She said something very like that again, to herself, as she stepped into her first-act costume: a robelike gown of white silk embroidered around the gracious hem, around the wide cuffs of the sleeves, and around the flattering neckline with gold and green and violet symbols of enslavement and freedom.

She took her time. She did not want her anticipation to result in a torn seam or a smudged cuff. She adjusted and fastened and smoothed the heavy folds of white silk for some fifteen minutes before she finally walked regally across the bedroom in order to consider her image in the full-length, multipaneled mirror. It would not have been unusual for this woman, at such a moment, to take pleasure in her work, to congratulate herself, privately, and say something like, "Muriel Fontaine, you're one hell of an artist." But not this time. She said nothing of the sort. She gazed at herself in the mirror for a long time, front, side, and back, and then she said, out loud, lingering on each syllable, in some other voice rich with passion and consequence: *"Celeste Aida!"*

After she'd given her statement, Maggie went up to the kitchen and made coffee. She returned to the basement carrying a tray crowded with coffeepot, cups, saucers, spoons, milk, and sugar cubes. She decided to speak "on a one-to-one basis" with the younger, blond detective, even though something about the way he carried himself suggested that he wasn't much of a dancer. She touched his arm and asked him if he'd seen the bag of groceries upstairs. "I'm no private eye or anything," Maggie said, "but maybe it's a clue. It's just sitting there by the front door with all this food in it, like they must have left in a hurry. It's okay if I touched it, isn't it?"

Sam stopped on his way home from work at a small market whose patrons were mainly farmers and those who, like Sam and Muriel, chose to "live way out." Along with fresh eggs and milk every day, the eclectic store featured a comprehensive selection of Italian wines, Southern fried chicken cooked right on the premises, and Syrian bread shipped up from Utica three times a week. Sam suspected that neither he nor Muriel would have any appetite to speak of, but he left the store, nevertheless, with a bottle of Chianti, some fried chicken, some bread, and two perfect pears. It was twilight when he arrived home and entered the reconstructed old farmhouse and saw the woman standing in the middle of all that space, in the half-light, under the open ceiling. He forgot about the bag of groceries he was carrying as he reached his arms out to her.

The blond detective's name turned out to be Earl. Earl watched Maggie's mouth move when she spoke to him. No one had ever looked at her mouth that way before. She couldn't tell whether or not she liked it. Earl told her that the bag of groceries probably wouldn't tell them much about what happened, but he'd look into it. Maggie blushed and turned her eyes away when Earl went on to say, "And you can touch anything at all you want as far as I'm concerned, Miss Evans."

Sam DiCielo would not have been able to explain to them what happened to the bag of groceries when he saw the woman standing there, center stage, in the semishadows. He had raised his arms and taken a step toward her as if the two of them had already been in the midst of a long and complicated ballet. Then suddenly he had turned and walked off toward the far end of the house. He had said nothing directly to the woman, though had she inclined her head in his direction she might have heard him say to himself the words *per te ho pugnato, per te ho vinto,* the words that belong to Radamès, the unhappy hero of Verdi's *Aida.*

Sam first learned those words in 1943 when he was required by his commanding officer to take a three-day vacation from the war and think about his attitude. But it was only partly his attitude that he thought about as he drove east from Naples and ended up at last in Avellino, a town he had seen once before—through the bombsight of his B-17. There were not many people left in Avellino when Sam arrived, but he came upon three families who lived together in what used to be a church. There were fifty-seven relatives in all, young and old, and they all insisted that he stay there with them for his three-day vacation from the war. They would give him the best place to sleep and good pieces of their hard Italian bread rubbed all over with garlic and olive oil. But he must stay, they told him. There had been no audience for months. Yet here they were, a makeshift opera company, the three families together—"to get us through this war," they explained. And though they had no orchestra, not one violin, and no costumes to speak of, and no sets, they would show Sam what could be done. He would see, they said. And he did.

Sam had listened to the opera on the radio back in the States. He could recognize most of the famous arias and duets. But he had never before seen an opera performed, nor had he ever experienced anything of its kind until he found himself in the dark ruins of the church in Avellino and felt himself transported by the three families' rendering of the tragedy of *Aida:* the extravagance, the solemnity, the pageantry, the suffering, the unfathomable love, all of it transformed him so that he forgot for a while where he was. And the two oldest men, Signor Fumista, ninety-one, and Signor Strappazo, ninety-four, imitated Verdi's aggressive trumpets and his doomed violins with such dignity and force that Sam forgot for a while that he had listened to the entire opera sung a cappella. When he made his good-byes to his hosts on the third day, Sam said to them, "Radamès knew who he was fighting for."

But the woman who had once been Muriel Fontaine had inclined her head in the other direction, toward the mute and immutable sphinx, so that she did not hear the man say to himself the words *per te ho pugnato, per te ho vinto.* Not yet. She did not even see the man who spoke those words until he returned to the vast and expectant room almost an hour later. And then she saw that he was attired, like herself, in a heavy white robe, and that he wore an elaborate belt, bejeweled with turquoise and with amethyst, that reached the floor although it twice encircled the flowing garment that revealed the man's broad chest and his brown, muscular arms. And she saw that he wore a warrior's silver bracelets around his upper arms but he carried no weapon, and she saw that he had adorned his head not with a helmet ready for battle but with a headband black as jet and soft as ostrich down. She raised her arms, like wings, as he had earlier raised his, and she reached out to the man who was not Sam DiCielo but her secret warrior-lover who must betray his love, and hers, or perish.

The man walked into the circle of moonlight in which she stood and he touched the tips of her outstretched fingers, and then he brought her hands to his lips and kissed them.

It was curtain time. They took their places as the prelude began to propound their fate and fill their stage with the rhythms of grief and desire. The lights came up slowly and cast a dim, mythic glow around the dark blue sphinx as the music came alive with voices that belied the mediation of recording equipment and mechanical devices. The man and the woman felt the intense and immediate presence of the orchestra just as they felt the ominous and immediate presence of the Egyptian princess Amneris, whose jealousy

would attempt to destroy them; and the anguished and immediate presence of ancient Amonasro, the Ethiopian king
separated from his daughter Aida by senseless war; and the
demanding and immediate presence of a populace more
hungry for victory than for peace, calling, shouting with its
music for *guerra, guerra, guerra!*

Once the two lead singers had begun to enact and thereby
consecrate the roles they had assumed, they found that, this
time, they could not stop. The music held them on the stage,
made them forget that there were exits and entrances, costume changes and lights to dim, made them stay and listen
to their story unfold in all its glorious, tragic excess of self-
ishness and sacrifice; made them hear, over and over, the
cries from every quarter for some sign of heavenly justice—a cry that finally emanated even from the jealous
Amneris. But justice of any kind refused to the end to mani-
fest itself.

At last, therefore, without protest or defense, Radamès of
Egypt accepted the fate he had chosen when he chose to
love Aida, daughter of Ethiopia's king. He stood resolute and
silent as the high priests of Isis condemned him to slow
suffocation in a vault below the earth, never again to rest his
eyes on his country, on his people, on the woman whose
love he would not renounce—so resolute that, at the thresh-
old of his underground tomb, he stopped, threw down the
warrior's bracelets he had worn with tormenting pride, and
glared into the faceless face of the midnight-colored sphinx,
whose indifferent gaze made Radamès almost happy to de-
scend into the dark alone.

But not alone. Aida was there, waiting in the shadows for the finale, longing for the lullaby of death that would free her love forever. She looked up past the lion's paws of the sphinx at the chill December night and joined her Radamès in a song of passionate resignation: *O terra, addio; addio, valle di pianti.*

Over dinner Saturday night at The Valley Inn, Earl the blond detective said to Maggie Evans, "I still can't figure out what went on out there. It's stranger than heck." Maggie nodded and said, "It sure is." She was thinking to herself, So is *this*—this last-minute date with a guy she barely knew. She thanked her lucky stars that she'd had time to go home after the investigation and change into something dressy and redo her hair. She liked the way it turned out. She had fashioned it into a bun on top of her head and then decorated it with a fancy comb of the sort worn by flamenco dancers. She could tell that Earl liked it, too, when he arrived to pick her up and said, "Well, hello there, señorita!"

Maggie watched Earl joke with the waiter. She loved the way he said the words *soave* and *veal parmigiano*. This is like a dream, she thought. She tried to remember her first impression of Earl, but she couldn't. There'd been too many other things going on.

It was as if Earl had been reading her mind. He bit off a piece of the breadstick he was holding and then he asked, "Do you believe in love at first sight? Across a crowded room? Somehow you just know?" Maggie smoothed the tablecloth, appraised the polish on her nails, and tried to compose herself. Earl finished his breadstick. He hoped he would not be drafted and sent to Vietnam before he and Maggie could get engaged. "Well, do you?" he asked her again. Maggie looked into his eyes. "I do," she said. And she added, "I feel pretty. Really pretty."

Red Horse Running Through Water

Every night for forty-four nights, after the men and the women had taken their empty plates back to the kitchen and had returned with steaming cups of coffee to their usual places in the dining hall, Jack tried to tell them the story, and for forty-four nights he could not tell it.

On the first night Jack began at what he thought was the beginning that would carry him straight and smooth to the end, and he said: This is the story of the death of Raymond White Eagle—perhaps you have heard his name when it is carried here to this faded desert settlement by the winds from the valley that smell of eucalyptus and something close to freedom.

But he could get only that far. The remaining words of the story refused to come forward. So Jack wrote down on a piece of paper that he felt as if a kumquat were stuck in his throat, and the piece of paper was passed from table to table, and the men and the women shook their heads in regret and nodded their heads in understanding and tried not to stare at Jack's throat, where indeed something like a kumquat appeared to be stuck.

Over the next few nights, a few sentences at a time, Jack was able to tell them some of the details of Raymond White Eagle's background, how he had been sent to a government boarding school called the Harmen Institute when he was a boy, but not as pliable a boy as the supervisors of his formal education might have liked. The thing about Raymond White Eagle, Jack told his captive audience, was that he was never one to let them see that he was not pliable in the least. So once he got his formal education, they kept him on at the Harmen Institute for many years—a grounds-keeper, they called him, since they did not know he was a teacher who showed us in secret how to listen to the voices of the Old Ones.

Ah, said the men and the women, and over those first few nights they began to forget how tiresome and salty their dinners often were because they got too busy thinking about the after-dinner story that Jack could not tell them from start to finish, and too busy wondering about the lump in Jack's throat, which had grown to about the size of a lemon.

At the beginning of the second week, one of the men suggested that instead of trying to tell his story from the same spot where he had just eaten his dinner, Jack should move to the front of the dining hall and tell it from there, and everyone approved of this idea with applause and nods and smiles. So two of the strong women picked up Jack's chair with Jack in it and carried it to the front of the room, whose old stucco walls did their best to contain and reverberate the laughter.

Jack told them that night, the eighth night of his trying, that after sixty-seven years Raymond White Eagle left the Harmen Institute, for he awoke one morning and found five albino eagle feathers on his windowsill, and they or the voices they represented or some new part of his old desire showed him the way to the burial grounds of his people. And he found that the graves were not covered with shopping malls or mobile homes but were deep in the valley beneath a green and white ranch where horses were raised and ridden for profit. And Raymond White Eagle became the fencekeeper at the horse ranch in the valley, and every day he walked miles of fence with a pail of paint and a hammer and nails, and while he kept the fence looking clean and straight and white, he spoke in old Shoshone to the Old Ones about all that had happened since they lost their land and died.

That was as far as Jack could get. It was not much, but he had made some progress, and the men and the women felt sure that Jack's move to the front of the dining hall had done him some good, that the lump in his throat was perhaps a little smaller—that in any case he had spoken to them for a longer time than ever before, and they were glad, for they believed that soon, perhaps tomorrow, they would learn the rest of the story about the man whose name is carried through the desert by the winds from the valley.

But Jack had a relapse. The next night he walked to the front of the dining hall after the tables had been cleared and the coffee had been poured and all he could say was, A red horse running through water. So he wrote down on a piece of paper that he was sorry, that he couldn't explain it, that he hoped to tell them soon what he meant, that he would not give up, no, and that he thought he ought to go to bed early. As his message was passed from table to table, Jack left the room almost unnoticed, but the others remained and drank coffee for hours and finally agreed on a way to help Jack tell the story he had come there to tell them, and someone was sent for the tools.

Late that night the rhythms of sawing and hammering escaped from the dining hall and danced upon the cool desert air and made the crickets dream the words to an ancient Chippewa chant.

On the tenth night of his telling, when he stepped onto the platform that the men and the women had built for him, Jack thanked them all and waved to the people in the back of the room—he could see them better now, he said, now that he had a platform to stand on. Then he squeezed a swallow past the lump in his throat and began: Tonight I am going to tell you about the man named Johnny Johnson. But the people moaned as if their voices were one and Jack had to stop and raise his hands, palms forward, in order to quiet the men and the women who had waited too long already, they said, to hear the story of Raymond White Eagle, and who had good reason, they said, to protest Jack's starting another tale about someone else. What about the red horse? one man asked.

Jack said, You'll see. And then he went on: One night, no, it was not night yet. It was close to sundown. I remember that it was not night because I remember that as I crossed the courtyard at the Harmen Institute where I too grew up and almost grew old, the chickens were one minute squawk-ing and the next minute sleeping. And they did not even get up on their roosts, as chickens must do, but plopped over like dogs and went to sleep before sunset with their ears to the ground.

Jack's audience responded to these details with audible oohs and aahs that made him feel better than he had felt in a long time.

And then the watcher, he told them, whose job it is to watch whoever tries to leave or enter the Harmen Institute, took off his uniform jacket and his uniform pants and took a walk toward the red setting sun. And then the hot dry wind that had been making the bougainvillea scrape and scratch against the wall of the dusty chapel for ten days and ten nights suddenly stopped. And the scraping and the scratch-ing stopped. Somewhere a train whistle stopped. And Ray-mond White Eagle stood under the arched entrance to the Harmen Institute where there was once a gate that had locked him in when he was a boy. I knew that it was him though he had been gone for three years and I had never seen him wear a hat like the one he was wearing—a cowboy hat, raven black, no, blacker than that, with a brim that curves downward in front, sharp, and a crown that is banded by an orange and yellow snakeskin. On one side of the brim are the five albino eagle feathers that are too white for a human being to look at for very long.

Jack stopped talking, but it was not clear whether he was finished for the evening or was catching his breath or was thinking about the hat, so the men and the women did not make a move until the oldest of the old women, who always sat at a table near the back with her seven daughters, came silently forward and handed Jack a glass of water.

And when he looked into her face, Jack said: I knew that it was Raymond White Eagle because his eyes were dangerous and holy and gray as the underpaws of the mountain lion. And still he wore his sideburns down to the bones of his jaw. And still he rolled long cigarettes that were as long as cigars. And when he stepped into my room that had once been his room at the Harmen Institute, Raymond White Eagle said to me, Johnny Johnson is waiting for us.

Johnny Johnson, said the men and the women.

Jack stepped down from his platform feeling drained, almost dizzy, and ashamed of himself for feeling so drained without having come close to the end of his story. But he smiled despite his shame and despite the pain that throbbed in his throat, for he saw that his people were content, or at least hopeful, as they said, Good night, Jack, sleep well.

But instead of sleeping well Jack wondered how much longer he could go on this way and he imagined, for a moment, the act of giving up. And when that moment was over he tried to convince himself that he could tell the whole thing in one or two more nights if he only put his mind to it and forgot everything else: forgot the thing in his throat that was getting to be the size of a nectarine, and forgot about telling the ending, and forgot about how he looked and how his hands moved like fish in a stream when he spoke in public, and forgot about how he couldn't control his tone, and forgot about the splendid, resonant, unhesitating voice of Raymond White Eagle, the first storyteller. Jack finally went to sleep saying to himself, I will do it, I'll do it tomorrow, and he dreamed of a red horse running through water, fast.

That same night the wind from the valley sailed into the desert and changed the minds of a pack of coyotes, who decided to leave their lonely arid hills and begin a new life among the people of the settlement, so they walked side by side toward the light that shone from the dining hall where the men and the women were again sawing and hammering and telling their dreams to one another until well after midnight.

From dawn until dark, every day of the week, Jack and the people of the settlement worked on the ditch that stretched toward the water that would turn their dry desert acres into a field of corn and beets. So Jack did not see until the next evening at suppertime that during the night they had built him a stage. There was no curtain, no backdrop, no props, no special lights—just three plain cedar walls and a cactus-bark roof with a fanciful pointed pitch to it. But a stage of sorts it was, and in its center was a lectern sculpted from a large piece of sandstone whose flakes of quartz made magic with the mundane lights in the dining hall. And when Jack finally did see the stageroomteepee that the men and the women had built for him, he was too filled with gratitude to say anything at all except, Thank you. And he returned to his room even earlier than usual and was glad the coyotes had warmed his bed.

Then it was the twelfth night and Jack felt strong and eager after his long sleep within the calm of dog. So when the evening meal was over he stepped buoyantly up to the new stage—as the men and the women had hoped he would—and he leaned his elbows on the lectern as if he had leaned them there many times before, and he said: Raymond White Eagle sat in the room that had once been his room and he smoked a long cigarette while he told me that the horse ranch in the valley where his people are buried is not the sort of horse ranch we might imagine, but a kind of school where the daughters of the white men who own things learned to ride expensive horses, and not ride them as we might imagine, but sideways and backwards and crossways in a dance with no purpose they called dressage—

Dressage, the men and the women repeated—
and they ride the horses over high fences as well, as high as the walls of this stage, for contests and for money. And the spirits of the Old Ones spoke to Raymond White Eagle about the many times they had helped the horses jump without harm the high piles of stones and logs, and they asked him why these horses had to leap so high for their keep: They are horses, said the Old Ones, they have no wings for flying. And Raymond White Eagle had tried to explain what little he knew about the white man's contests and taxes and investments, but the Old Ones did not see the reason. And the daughters, Jack continued, the girls who were not quite girls and not women either, were not what we might imagine, for each kept to herself and thought only of winning and did not share secrets with friends for they had none, not until things changed.

Jack took a long breath that was meant to give him time
to remember what came after "not until things changed."
But he had forgotten the words or had dropped them somewhere, and he looked around behind him as if he might
learn there what it was he was supposed to say next. Oh yes,
he mumbled with his back to his audience. But he did not
mean Oh yes at all—instead he meant Oh no. For he had
lost his story, that was clear, and he could not find it no
matter how hard he stared at the floor or the walls or the
fanciful ceiling above his head. It was gone. All Jack could
find were some fragments, bits and pieces, here and there,
eighteen of them altogether. I could spread them out over
eighteen nights, Jack said to himself, thinking fast. Maybe by
then I will find the rest, maybe by then I'll remember. So for
the next eighteen nights Jack offered what he could, a piece
at a time, and it went like this:

Johnny Johnson horseman manhorse (That's all, Jack said,
and the people said, That's all right).

Girls blond frowning private (and the people, after Jack
was gone, elected the man with the most beautiful handwriting to write down the fragments Jack managed to tell
them).

Eucalyptus trees undressing (Jack said twice, but the men
and the women agreed that the repetition, in this case, did
not seem to matter).

Flared nostrils like deer (and Jack flared his nostrils in
order to show the people what he meant).

Raymond White Eagle saw (and the people repeated *he
saw,* and they gave each other understanding looks since

they knew by then that if there were something to see Raymond White Eagle was likely to see it).

Manhorse whinnying pawing the earth (then Jack sat with a cup of hot chocolate while the men and the women demonstrated whinnying and pawing and talked about how a man with the name Johnny Johnson might do such things).

La Traviata Calypso King Red Thunder (and the people threw up their hands and said, Impossible, until one of the seven daughters of the oldest old woman whispered to her friend that if she had a horse she would name it Red Thunder).

Circling pretending the girls (and the men and the women said, Those girls again).

You lucky dog (Jack said with a curious smile on his face).

Red horse running through water (said Jack, and he looked so tired that the men and the women did not try to keep him from returning quickly to his room).

Sunday morning (Jack began, and then he took a breath and added:) repudiation Sunday (and after he had said those four words he leaned against the lectern for an hour and thirty-five minutes on the eleventh of the eighteen nights).

Raymond White Eagle saw (and the people asked the man with the most beautiful handwriting to put a special mark next to this fragment because this, they believed, was no mere repetition).

Leaning into his scent picnics for grooms (and that night everyone, including Jack, ate second helpings of dessert beneath the bright desert stars).

Imported teachers of dressage (and again the people repeated in unison the word *dressage*).

Linking arms a ring (Jack said to the men and the women with his arms outstretched).

What dream (said Jack, and then for a while he held his head in his hands).

The hat (he whispered, and the people knew which hat he meant, the black one, and some had even seen the hat when they had visited Jack in his room).

Old Ones desire (Jack said on the eighteenth night).

Jack stayed later than he usually did in the dining hall that night and listened to the men and the women discuss the bits of story he had told them thus far, and he felt the lonesomeness that has to do with missing oneself. But as he walked to his room around midnight he was able to make the sentence, *The Old Ones filled the valley with desire,* and he kept on repeating the sentence to himself so that he would not lose it and would not have to think about the rest of the story that seemed to be lost forever. But when he entered his room, he saw it. It was sleeping half-hidden among the pile of suckling coyote pups that had been born on his blanket nearly three weeks before, and Jack understood why his story had abandoned him for this, and he did not blame it since he would probably get in there too if he could.

Jack began the thirty-first night of trying to tell the story he could not tell by announcing to his people that the story had been found, that their patience would be rewarded— but perhaps not right away, he added, especially since the thing in his throat was now as large as an avocado and it, or something else that Jack could not name, was changing the sound of his voice, making it deeper, slower, older. So for tonight, he said to his audience, I can only tell you, I will tell you about, let me start over. Jack went through the motions of clearing his throat that could not be cleared and then he said: Johnny Johnson came to the valley from the east and the west and the north and the south and he had no car and no watch and no money and no desire for cars or watches or money, and he had no past and no present worth knowing, but he could talk to a horse better than some horses can talk to each other. And this horseman Johnny Johnson paid no mind to the daughters of the owners as they pouted and eyed him and then turned their eyes to the ground, but Raymond White Eagle saw it all from the first day Johnny Johnson showed up like a dandelion out of nowhere. He saw the noses of the girls flare like the noses of deer as they breathed in the smell of Johnny Johnson, and he saw how up and down the length of the barn the horses hung their heads out over the doors of their stalls and stretched toward Johnny Johnson as he read the names from the brass plates nailed to each door—La Traviata, Calypso King, Red Thunder, and all the other names. And he saw Johnny Johnson hug their necks and rub their foreheads and their eyes while the girls circled and watched and pretended not to watch or circle, and pretended not to see that wherever Johnny Johnson walked the dust became pungent and wet, and pretended not to hear him snort and whinny and then paw the earth and call himself a lucky dog. What a lucky dog I am, Johnny Johnson said to Raymond White Eagle. I'm home, said Johnny Johnson. And then—

Jack could not go on. Something pulled him back to the words *I'm home.* He wanted to go forward, to get to the next sentence and the next one after that, but something else wanted him to go backward, to say *I'm home.* I will have to stop now, Jack said to himself, though he found that in fact he had spoken out loud, for he heard his people saying, Yes, why don't you stop now, do not tire yourself, we can wait. We have a present for you. And they handed him a blanket that was the color of the first desert sunset and was embroidered with the eighteen fragments he had spoken on the eighteen nights he had tried to tell the story even though it was hiding from him. And that night and every night thereafter Jack wrapped himself in the bluegreenyelloworangepurple blanket and the sentences he could not make and he never had a bad dream again.

For the next seven nights Jack said to himself that it was all right that he was not able to tell the story as he had intended to tell it, the way Raymond White Eagle would tell it—without a breath, sweeping along like the wind from the valley, gathering and embracing but never pausing, always moving, always sweeping toward the sea. It was all right, Jack told himself again and again. People are different. I cannot be him. I will tell the story a few minutes at a time. That is all someone like me can do. And the men and the women cleared the tables and brought in steaming cups of coffee, knowing as Jack knew that it was not really all right, that it would not be all right until Jack could soar through each note of his story and wear the hat that was raven black, no, blacker than that, which he kept on a table in his room.

But the men and the women and Jack himself made believe that Jack's way of telling was the best way for him. And so for a week, a few minutes at a time, Jack told them about the turbulence of the girls that no one saw at first except Raymond White Eagle; and he told them about the scent of Johnny Johnson, which was the scent of saddle and alfalfa and cheap cologne, and how the girls and then their mothers leaned into the scent of Johnny Johnson and changed their minds, so that their minds might be more like what they thought his was; and he told them how the girls and their mothers brought grand picnics for the grooms and the field hands and asked them to sit in the shade of the eucalyptus trees and eat; and while the grooms and the field hands ate, the girls and their mothers curried and brushed the horses for the first time, and they rubbed the horses' legs with liniment and scraped manure from their hooves for the first time; they tied their blond hair in bandanas and cleaned the stalls and the saddles and the bridles and drove the tractors loaded with irrigation pipes for the first time; and Jack told them how the girls for the first time ever opened the gates and rode off into the hills; and then he told them how the fathers came to the horse ranch in the valley to look things over and to worry out loud about the land they possessed and the investments they had made in horses and arenas and imported teachers of dressage, and to ask out loud of the girls and their mothers, What has happened here to the Spirit of Competition? And Jack told them that when Johnny Johnson walked by he stopped to find out if any of them— the girls or their mothers or their fathers—had seen how the eucalyptus trees shed their bark in such large smooth pieces, It's kinda like they're taking off their clothes, don't ya think? And Jack said that when Raymond White Eagle spoke to him of all these things he was grinning the grin of one who knows where the thing is buried that he has been looking for for a long time.

Ah, said the people.

And when the week was over the men and the women came up to the stage and touched Jack's arms and squeezed his callused hands in theirs and spoke words of praise and comfort. And though the lump in his throat now looked to be the size of a grapefruit, Jack did not think to cover it, for he was more than a little elated by the approval of his people, and a flush came into his cheeks that remained there for days.

It was November—no one could have foreseen the coming of the awful heat that for the next several days fell upon the settlement like a proprietary giant who does not look about him before he lies down and goes to sleep. No one said that the heat that had never before paid them a November visit had anything to do with Jack's half-told story. The heat has simply lost its way, they said as they worked on their ditch that was now over four miles long, only one half mile away from the mountain where the scouts had found a stream that would turn their dry desert acres into a field of corn and beets. Soon the heat will wake up and remember where it is supposed to be this time of year, the people said as they returned to the settlement scorched and exhausted at the end of the day, far too worn out to listen to any storytelling, especially Jack's kind of storytelling.

But Jack was flushed and relaxed and too dazed from the heat to recall his limitations. He was ready, he thought, to get to the end, to finish. I could tell it all, Jack said to himself, tell it all without a breath. But now they cannot hear me. So from the sandstone lectern he looked out upon the vague rounded shapes that the imperial heat had made of his audience and he spoke to them briefly about the short half mile they had left to dig and he wished them a good night's rest, but they were asleep in their chairs before he finished even that.

For five days and five nights the heat lay heavily upon the settlement, making the people dizzy and furious and mute, until it finally awoke, as they knew it would, and left under cover of darkness without apology, as they knew it would.

On the next day, the forty-fourth day, the sky that framed Jack and his people as they dug toward the mountain looked like cool blue water, and the breeze brought them odors of pine and mesquite that banished their aches and their silence. And they finished all but the last few yards of the digging before they hurried back to the settlement for a night of celebration and feasting, for the oldest of the old women had gone that day with her daughters into the forest on the mountain and had returned with dozens of silky rainbow trout and with necklaces for everyone made of juniper and holly berries, and with pine boughs and ferns to decorate Jack's stage. (These adornments will raise expectations, Jack said to himself, and then he added, Don't worry. You'll do fine.)

But even before the special meal was over, long before the plates were returned to the kitchen and the coffee cups brought out, Jack found a piece of paper and wrote, The lump in my throat, it is worse. I may have trouble when it is time for me to speak. Remember that the Old Ones filled the valley with desire. And the men and the women handed the note from table to table and smiled encouragement at Jack, though they wondered how he would be able to get any words at all past the thing in his throat that was larger than ever, and they saw that Jack was wondering the same thing when later he stood on the stage strewn with pine boughs and ferns and said nothing for twenty minutes. Then one of the women began to chant: The Old Ones filled the valley with desire. The Old Ones filled the valley with desire. Everyone joined in, gently, almost whispering, and when they were about to finish saying the words for the seventh time, Jack blurted out, *with desire:* Johnny Johnson for the horses, the girls for Johnny Johnson, the mothers for they knew not what, for wind and pasture and work, Raymond White Eagle for a place beside his people, and all of them for the smell of the eucalyptus trees—

Yes, said the people, and Jack took a breath—
and when the fathers went again to the ranch to look things over and announce their worries, the wind from the valley began to blow and blow, and it blew the fathers up onto a ridge from which they could see all the land they owned for miles and miles. And then the wind blew them down so that they lay next to the earth on the graves of the Old Ones, who sang for them the ancient song of repudiation and munificence. And in the early evening when the wind finally stopped the fathers walked close together back to the barn where the others were waiting, and then the fathers relinquished the land and the horses and the arenas and the imported teachers of dressage. They relinquished and con-

veyed it all to the mothers who turned it over to the daughters who gave it all to Johnny Johnson who offered it to Raymond White Eagle who would not own it—

No, he would not, said the men and the women—

Raymond White Eagle would not own the land, Jack continued, but he wished to be buried there. Which is why he came back to the Harmen Institute and took me with him to the valley in the green truck that Johnny Johnson drove, and why he told Johnny Johnson the story of the Old Ones and their Dance of Life and why he asked Johnny Johnson to tell it to the others so they would know what to do when the time came, and they did.

Jack took a deep breath and rubbed his throat and tried not to feel the gaze of the oldest old woman whose gray eyes were the eyes of Raymond White Eagle and whose gaze embraced Jack as if he were her child or her father. Then he said: Raymond White Eagle told me that I would not return to the Harmen Institute and that I would find my home in the desert near the mountain where I would hear his name carried by the wind from the valley and where I would tell you all—

Jack stopped. The oldest old woman, who was older than Raymond White Eagle was at the time he decided to die, came forward without a sound and stepped onto the stage and lightly kissed Jack on the mouth. Then she returned without a sound to her place beside her daughters near the back of the dining hall.

Where I would tell you all, Jack went on, that I saw in the valley on a Sunday morning, on the day after Raymond White Eagle could no longer tell his own story, I saw them all, arms linked in a ring, singing to the sun and to the eucalyptus trees and to the rich brown color and the sweet supple smell of the upturned earth on the slope of pasture where Raymond White Eagle is buried.

Jack gasped for breath. He could not continue. The lump in his throat felt as if it were moving. And Jack was so startled that he suffered almost no pain as the thing moved slowly into his mouth, and then he cried out once and it dropped into his waiting hands, which were ready to catch it even though Jack could not believe that there would really be something to catch. But there was, and he caught it, and he held it up for the people to see.

The next day the water came to the settlement from out of the stream on the mountain, down through the five-mile ditch, and the first thing the men and the women planted was the seed that Jack had given birth to. Some said the seed was shaped like a watermelon, others that it was perfectly round; some said that you could see right through it, others that it was surely opaque; some said that it was silveryblue, others that it was yelloworange. Those who said that by springtime the seed will have become a tree that would shed its bark in large smooth pieces and bear fourteen different kinds of fruit for a hundred years or more were right. And when the people of the settlement linked arms and sang and danced around the spot where the seed was buried, they asked Jack, Is this how they danced and sang, the people in the valley who learned from Johnny Johnson who learned from Raymond White Eagle how to listen to the music of the Old Ones? Is this how they danced and sang? And Jack said, Yes, that is how.

And that night after the tables had been cleared and the coffee had been poured, Jack put on the hat and leaned against the lectern, and he saw in the faces of his audience that he wore the hat of Raymond White Eagle as if he had worn it all along. And in his new voice, a voice that was resonant and unhesitating and splendid, he told them everything again without a breath from beginning to end, and he did not leave out the eighteen fragments, for they had become part of the story, part of Jack's way of telling it. And when he came to the last words, *where Raymond White Eagle is buried,* he paused. Then he said, There is more—

Yes, said the people. There is the red horse.

So Jack told the men and the women that it was on the second day after Raymond White Eagle brought me to the valley so that I might witness the end of his story—he was already awake and dressed when the fingers of the sun began to reach over the horizon and take hold of the sky. Good-bye Jack, Raymond White Eagle said to me in the language of the Old Ones. And I said to him, I thought you would go into the sleep last night that one does not wake up from. That is the usual way, according to the voices you taught me to hear. But Raymond White Eagle shook his head and smiled, and you would have seen in the way he shook his head and smiled and in the talking of his hands and in the darkness of his eyes that he welcomed his death even though he had not let himself go into the sleep that one does not wake up from.

Then in the peachpurple light of early morning, I walked with him to the barn and he asked me, What dream do you have that makes you want to leap into the dream and stay there? And I told him, I dream of riding a red horse running through water, fast. And Raymond White Eagle said, So do I. And that is what he did that day until his heart stopped—

And it was glorious, said the people.

Yes, said Jack. It was.

From You Know Who

That sneaky old Lilly had been reading the letters for near up to three months before she got the nerve to tell me about them. As if I would ever confiscate them for no reason! You can bet I told her that her not sharing them right off was a shameful thing. Here we've been under this same roof over seventy years, but she acts sometimes like she doesn't know who I am. So I gave her a rough piece of my mind about it, even though I know she got that fear about her private things being confiscated from our father. He once even confiscated our schoolbooks, we never did know why. It got to where Lilly and me were digging holes out back near the cherry orchard in order to save things.

Richard hid things too, only nowheres near the orchard. Lilly said she found the letters in a cave too small for a person my size to crawl into, over on the hill some folks call Rock Ridge but we personally (meaning me and Lilly and Richard) always called Heath's Cliff after that book of Emily Brontë's that our mother read to us more than once when we were small.

The letters were all tied up in neat bundles, stored in old coffee cans, and just left there in the cave. Lilly showed me how she was still keeping them in the cans, all lined up on a shelf in her room like encyclopedias. But I made her throw those rusty old cans away and keep the letters in the special box that we used for the good silverware until we sold it all. The box is lined inside with purple velvet that I like to run my fingers over whenever I take the letters out or put them back.

Richard was born after Lilly and me. She was first, then me two years later, then Richard five years after that. Our mother, her name was Daphne—that's a name I like—she died when Richard was four or so, they didn't know from what. Father said we weren't to speak of it. Before she died she said to me, "Edith, you and Lilly take good care of your brother." So we threw ourselves hog-wild into pampering him. He was the prettiest and the sweetest-natured boy you'd ever want to meet. We keep a picture of him over there on top of the piano from when he was seventeen or thereabouts, not too long before he went over to that war and got killed by some people we'd never heard of. I forget now what they were called. But it doesn't matter, I guess, since somebody told us that country doesn't exist anymore anyway.

From the letters we got the idea that this girl of his had a picture of him too. Probably like the one we have, it's such a handsome rendering of Richard's smile. Like a cat holding a live dragonfly in its mouth, about to let it go. Surely he gave her some picture just like it. I would have, if it'd been me. Folks around here figured that secret look in his brown eyes meant he'd grow into a poet or some such type of person. That's what they said, though to my personal knowledge Richard never did write a stitch of anything his whole life.

That girl of his is another story. When Lilly first let me in on the letters, I told her the girl wrote enough to keep a whole roomful of lovers good and busy for weeks. Keep them all out of trouble, I told her. I was teasing, of course, but Lilly wouldn't have any of it, as usual. She got on me right away, all long-windedly. Called me Edith May Martin, my whole name, to let me know she was good and mad. Said I had the dirtiest mind she ever met or ever thought to meet in an old woman. A woman twice as old as those scraggily old apple trees we can see from the front porch. She said I was scragglier. Worse than that was her saying she had a mind not to let me see any more of those letters. Finders are keepers in this world, she told me.

I could see right then and there by the uppity way she talked that Lilly and me were likely to have some indecorous dealings over those letters. It plain wasn't right the way she claimed to be the boss over them. But back then I thought I'd best be circumspectful and kindly around her as much as I could. There looked to be near five hundred letters to read. It wasn't until later that I found out there's exactly six hundred and twelve, but I knew after I'd had a taste of the first few of them that I needed to read the rest. Had to. 'Course I didn't breathe a word of my having-to to Lilly. I just knew that I needed to read those letters the way some folks I've heard of need to slip any old object into their pocket every time they drop over to the five-and-dime. Can't help it.

This girl wrote to Richard sometimes up to three letters a day. Each one's the same. She always squeezed her longings onto a piece of plain white paper, five-inch by seven-inch, according to my measuring. At the top she'd put Monday Morning or Monday Evening, but never any dates. Never signed her name. Lilly said it didn't matter about the dates because Richard would have kept them all in order, week by week. I myself wasn't so ready to see him as being all that tidy a man. So we'd disagree now and again, me and Lilly, about what goes where. But that wasn't near as bad as when we got to arguing about what they meant. Lord. I'll show you what I mean. Here's one we never did see eye-to-eye on. I don't believe we ever could.

Tuesday Afternoon

Richard darling—

I still have the smell of your hair and your skin trapped here in my hands. So I opened up my fist just a tiny bit to let the pen in. I need more than ever to write to you after we've been so close that way. I do love you so. The times between the times when we're together go so slowly they would surely come in last against a snail. The way you touched the bottom of my foot, do you remember? I keep on feeling the broad smooth tips of your fingers on me. I love that it's getting to be that we talk more now. I have to know all there is to know about you, inside and out, and I know you want the same. We are one in body and spirit and always will be forever.

from You Know Who

You can see for yourself what a ninny Lilly was about this letter. To my mind, it's plain as soup that Richard and this You Know Who girl were full lovers, that's what I'd call them. When she says here "so close that way" I know enough to know which way she means. It's as close as a woman can get with a man. I tried to get Lilly to see how the girl makes no bones about saying that they'd been doing a whole lot of something that's not talking. Then I said how I liked that part about the foot, but the part about the pen was all silliness, seems to me.

Lilly was all the while turning purple as a turnip left too long in the ground. She said there was nothing specified about them being full lovers. That's what a ninny she is, like I told you. As far as she's concerned, it's all in my mind, which is a dungheap. She tried to show me how it was all spiritual. That when the girl writes about them being one in body it's only a manner of speaking. Same as when they talk about us eating the body of Christ and don't mean that at all. Lilly acted as if the case was closed when she said, "and besides, this letter was written on Tuesday *afternoon.*" To her this meant that the two of them would have been doing their whatnot in the morning. And that's an idea Lilly can't think of and never will.

But I'll tell you, it makes sense to me. There were some mornings out there on our hill—it's been years and years since I was up there. On some of those mornings there'd be a perfectly middling breeze, the kind that sways right there between cool and warm, and now and again presses your skirt against your legs. New sunlight would seem about to

lick the petals clean off the stems of the violets. It would
have been on such a morning. I can't see the wrongness of
it. Depends on how you look at a thing. After all, I said to
Lilly, when it's morning in Vermont, it's nighttime in China
far as I know. But Lilly just shook her head. Then she packed
up the letters and wouldn't let me see any again for a week.
Not a one.

I calculated the whole thing between Richard and that girl
lasted about eight months altogether, right up to his going off
in the winter sometime. Father had already gone off, I remember, and left us to ourselves. I won't say abandoned.
He'd come around every so often, we didn't know from
where. Besides, me and Lilly were over twenty by then. The
last time we saw him was after we'd gotten word about our
brother, how he'd been killed over there. They never did tell
us what killed him or why they couldn't send the body back.
We thought maybe Father knew, but we didn't ask him.
Father had got some money somehow, more than he ever
thought he'd have, in connection with the war. He gave us
enough so we could pay off the farm and go on living here.
He didn't want our thanks, he said. We never could figure
him out. He confiscated even on that last day. Went on into
our rooms and took up the little bit of jewelry our mother
left with us. He said unmarried women didn't need any
jewelry. And no one would want to marry us anyhow. I
guess he was right.

According to that girl of Richard's, marrying wasn't all that
needful for a woman. She told him as much. Must have been
he was feeling on edge about them not being married. It
would be just like him to worry about not offending, doing

what others wanted. He once told Lilly and me, a long time ago, after dinner one night, I think—yes, it was after dinner, and we'd eaten some pheasant he'd brought home that same afternoon, and Lilly cooked up the best stuffing we ever ate. It was nobody's birthday, but it seemed like it that night. Anyway, Richard said it was positively proper we weren't married because no man in our whole neck of the woods was worthy of either one of our hands in matrimony. Told us we were both princesses in a land of dullards and brutes. That's how he talked. So high-minded and poetical. I can't help but wish I'd seen his face when his girl wrote and told him she wasn't fretting over marriage. Wouldn't do it if she could, I suspect. I'll show you what I mean. Look here.

Thursday Evening

Dearest Richard—
Let us dream exactly the same dream tonight, and it won't resemble the dreams of any others. We're not like them at all, so we won't dream about fancy clothes or churches or new luggage that would make diminished stories of our vows. I know you know this is true, even though I could almost taste the concern that settled in around your eyes this afternoon when we spoke of it. And it was like the taste of aniseed. When I am with you tomorrow I will lick whatever's left away, then kiss your eyes while you unbraid my hair. We are one and I am with you always.

from You Know Who

This girl flies in the face of everything a body could suppose a girl to want. But I didn't say so to Lilly. She'd find some way to turn Miss You Know Who's gumption into something ordinary as oatmeal. It was getting to where I hadn't the stomach anymore for my sister's watered-down versions of things. So I kept the not-marrying business to myself. Let Lilly twist it into whatever she wanted.

But I couldn't keep mum about everything. It was when we'd gotten up to the two hundred and fourteenth letter that I decided to bring out into the light of day how curious it was that Richard was able to see so much of this girl, he needing to be here for chores most of the time and all. Lilly gave me one of those narrow looks of hers and asked me what I was insinuating. That's the exact word she used. Insinuating. But I was careful not to get worked up over it. For all I know, if I said the wrong thing, Lilly would take those letters, lock herself up with them, and throw the key into some crack in the wall. So I said, "I was only speculating, that's all," in about as sugary a voice as I could. "It seems that girl must have had a place close by," I told her. "Maybe she fixed herself up some sort of quarters out at the far silo. Maybe so, don't you think, Lilly?" But she wouldn't answer. Just stared at me hard as nails. Like she always does when she thinks I'm lying about something or other.

We'd been reading seven letters a day every day except Sunday. That's how Lilly determined we'd read them. She kept the key to the mahogany box on a dang-blasted chain that had to be unclasped each time since it wouldn't slip over her head. After breakfast she would stroll over to the box—it sits all by itself there on the buffet. Then she would unlock it. Then she would take out exactly seven letters, which she said followed the ones we'd read the day before.

She wouldn't change this procedure one iota. And she always got to hold the letters in her lap. Said I wasn't to be trusted with more than one at a time. I never have been able to figure out what she thought I'd make happen if I held two of those letters at once. But there was no reasoning with her. She allowed that we could read the seven over again as many times as we wanted during the day, long as chores got done. But the reading had to stop at suppertime. No looking at them in the evening. No reading by candlelight. Lilly eats that way too, in tiny bites, always saving something up, the best parts, for later, for tomorrow or some other day.

She's spoken hardly a word to me since I took over the management of the letters. The box, the key, the schedule, the whole kit-and-caboodle. And I'll tell you, I haven't tried more than what's reasonable to make up with her. For all I know, she kept the letters all to herself those first three months so she could read every darn one of them privately, anytime she chose. Out of spite or I don't know what kind of meanness she put us on that seven-a-day system in order to torture me. Pay me back. So I didn't even tell her that I got part of the idea of how to get some say-so about the letters from Miss You Know Who herself. I've got them all right here. Yessir. Here's the one I borrowed some of her gall from.

Saturday Evening

Richard my love—
Late this afternoon after you walked away with a golden sliver of straw wrapped up in your brown curls I found the key to

Miller's storage shed. It's so full of things to eat it's hard to choose. He discovered me there but he knows I know his secrets so he'll do nothing, there's nothing he can do but let me go there now and then. So in the morning when the first light begins to press itself against my door I want to open it and find you standing there. And I'll have a surprise—a breakfast of four fresh eggs, a hunk of deep orange cheese, two apples, almost purple. We are we forever.

from You Know Who

When I was sure I'd burn up and disappear into a puff of smoke if I had to sit with those measly seven letters one more time, I one morning just up and snatched the key away, chain and all, as Lilly was about to open the box. I remember trembling something awful, like a wet dog, from the grabbing and then hearing my sister scream some words at me that I didn't even know she knew. It turned out her palm was cut pretty deep from trying to hold onto the chain. But I was afraid to help her tend it, knowing she might try to get the best of me. I figured I better do first things first. Put the plan I got from that letter into effect. Quiet and serious as a judge I said to Lilly, "You've had your turn. Now it's mine. And if you try to do anything to upset this new arrangement we've made, I'll tell everyone some secrets about you that you don't want known." All she said back was that I was an incestuous monster. She went out of the room and I didn't see her again until the next day. Which was fine with me. When I opened that box for the first time all by myself I kept thinking about what that girl wrote about its being so full of things to eat it's hard to choose.

It could be you're thinking that me and Lilly are always unkind to each other. Sometimes we might have done things we aren't proud of. I'm not one to pull the wool over it. We've been mainly civil though, all these years. Mainly civil, but not what you'd think of as close friends. Mine for the longest time was Sandra Lynn Hopper, until she got married when she was twenty-eight to a gentleman-farmer named Sorenson Lee. They weren't married for too long, I heard, before he shot her in the stomach and went off to St. Louis. But Lilly and me have always been together, right here, day in and day out. Went to the same school and all. But didn't talk all that much about things. Seems as if early on we knew we were different as could be. She doesn't know this, mind you, but if I had to keep my promise and send out word about her secrets, I'd be put to shame. I was only guessing that after all this time on earth she'd have at least one thing she doesn't want the world to hear about. I have a secret or two myself, of course, but chances are they're not worth telling.

After Lilly stormed out of the room that morning, first I fixed the broken chain so I could wear the key around my own neck. Then I read letter after letter. All day. And stayed up all night to finish them. Then I started over again from the beginning. Around lunchtime the next day Lilly came out. She was wearing our mother's blue robe. She said, "What's your hurry?" That's all. You can bet I didn't see any reason to answer such a ragged-ended question as that. Besides, my mind was feeling pretty disorganized from all that reading.

It still strikes me as curious how I get so flustered up reading the letters. Richard's girl, even when she's writing about his going off to war, stays peaceful as that loaf of bread cooling off by the sink. Don't know how she does it. I'll give you a for instance from one of these last letters. Here she talks some about Richard's hair—I wonder he never got tired of her doting on his hair. Then she goes on calm as could be about this fellow named Avery who'd been killed in some other war, seems like.

> Avery took a lucky charm with him when he rode off to the war on his high-stepping chestnut mare. It was the greenest clover leaf caught forever inside a teardrop of sap, near the size of a rosebud, that had hardened after a while and was like glass. He used to hold it in his palm and rub it with his thumb and fingers over and over, and we'd beg for a turn, and he'd say children don't need such luck, especially girls. But his charm didn't save him after all, the way my love will save you and bring you back whole, breathing that same sweet breath you tickle my skin with. . . .

I got this idea she might be related somehow or other to one of the Averys. There's plenty of them around here, used to be, at least. Maybe she got her calmness from them. I said so to Lilly while she was making herself a cup of tea. But she pretended not to hear me. I went ahead anyway and spoke what was on my mind. Which was that Richard's girl might still be alive, close by, grieving her heart into dust. And that we ought to look her up, locate her, I told Lilly, through one of those Averys. "Maybe she'd like to know us," I said, "us being the sisters of Richard and all. Even though it's been more than fifty years. I know sure as I live that our girl would never have taken up with someone else. It's too deep." Lilly just drank her tea. Didn't offer me any. So I went on. "Since you and me aren't fit for traipsing around the countryside, why don't I ring up MaryJane, over to the post office, and see if she'll give us a hand? Help us find the whereabouts of this girl?" It was like I was talking clean out loud to no one, doing all the planning by myself. Lilly just sat there like an old statue, except for those measly tears of hers that came out of one eye, then the other, and landed in her lap.

Olé, Henry!

*"But what is it you've in mind that
I may have a chance to sacrifice?"*

"Oh one has always something."

—Henry James, "The Tree of Knowledge"

. . . Her thing with Henry began *in medias res,* when soon-to-be Gloria was more or less in graduate school at NYU, verging virginally on thirty, going by the name of Ricky or sometimes Rickety, her hair wild, red, her clothes ranch-style bohemian, her demeanor incognito and incommunicado, her essays all in one way or another about the fleetingness of phallic images, her favorite pastime Observation, which came in handy when she came upon Henry and began to spend her evenings reconstructing the moment when Henry would have come upon her.

As it were. For as it was old Henry was a hardbound nut to crack, though on behalf of his deportment (of which he had *mucho*) she called herself Gloria, dressed her Brooklyn cowgirl lankiness in loose Italian white, and resisted the temptation to poke fun at his reserve, to poke him indiscreetly and provoke what would have been a masterful clearing of his throat, such was her gratitude for the sense of belongings that his words wrapped her up in, such was her passion for the nimble subtlety with which he encoded the possibilities, the handy way he handled his tool, the circumloquacious phrase.

Bon appétit!

She ate him up, devoured the words that were all that remained of the secretly salty Henry, her altar of the dead a dining-room table piled high and then higher with the tantalizing object of her interpretive advances. He was the corpus delectable, the discursive body with whom she could mean but needn't be, and Gloria took him in (did she ever), savoring more than anything else all those Henrified slow-cooked phrases that refused to commit, make vows, name names, tell truths, or otherwise invest in living others.

Outfaced and o'ermatched by Henry's eloquent daring and double-daring of desire, Gloria fell in something very like love, parked her boat in his portly port, gave herself over to tongue-tied intercourse in between yes and no, dead and alive, *Ding* and dong. So she subdued her hair and kept her head, kept it poised and more or less transparent for Henry's gray omniscient eye, refined her tastes, attended her courses, wrote a thesis on the role of figurines in the nineteenth-century sentimental novel, and taught herself badminton—the perfect game, she thought, that quiet shuttlecock, gentle enough to be played indoors, dressed up for tea, a sport for interior paramours.

In time, as questions of wherewithal are bound to arise, she married an aged financeer named Phillip (a petered-out replica of her younger brother—the other, fundless Phillip) who grew exceedingly fond of Henry, would wrestle his wife for possession, so fond indeed that as he breathed his last fulsome breath, not two years after he had betrothed himself to the necessarily faithful Gloria, it was Henry's name that he spoke.

It had always been like that, Henry's name on lips other than hers, her unpuckered mouth rivaled by wordmongers who claimed Henry for their own, especially a woman named Cynthia who would always go by that name and of whom it was rumored that she was Henry's daughter. But Gloria knew better. Henry, in so many words, was all hers. She lived with him for ten years or more, traveled at his corpulent side, observed his observations, mirrored the texture of his regrets, his little triumphs over the trickiness of touching, the circuitous pleasure he no doubt took in his afternoon naps. Her head would turn in sync with his to face the wall, a parabolic pas de deux, a preemptive rejection of rejection, as comforting as coin, as sweet as sacrifice.

. . . Then one icy morning when the leafless trees spoke to her in a lumbering sort of way about quiddities and quests, Gloria's composure caved in under the dead weight of ever-miscalculated intimacy. She sensed, of course reluctantly, that it was time to close the book on her affair with Henry, to select a memento (he would have called it something exceptional, something peculiarly *hers*) and move out of those rooms overburdened with things that mattered—in none of which had she ever had so much as a peek at the hairs on Henry's chest, if there were hairs to see, despite her devotion to fine art and to the fine art of the erotic unsaid word, the thing unnamed which Gloria once, early on in the relationship, when she was still unschooled enough to have mistaken her passion for power, *had* named, had seen herself whisper into Henry's flaky ear, her hand resting on his neopolitan paunch in such a way that he might or might not know it was there. She had said the word, two words in fact, her glorious cheekbones hot with the risk of it, two words of which Henry would have made a note, ignoring the hand encurled in his watch chain, then written a sentence, and then another, and then a story, a stuttering waltz of words, an almost but never quite coupling crowd of words, not one sluttish word among them, nothing untoward, which, after all, was one of the things the ungestalted Gloria had always loved about Henry—the ponderous delicacy with which he sipped his tea and zipped his trousers and pressed his thoughts upon the costs of staying alive.

So she had hung in there, had hung out with Henry, so continent and oh so continental, until the trees that encircled her garden, trees not destined for the paper mill, for book-dom, for the riddledom of a tenacious teasing pen, let her know that she was aging, that it was time to throw in the guest towel, turn the page, move to her brother Phillip's place in the mountains of Colorado and change her name to Filomena.

*   *   *

. . . Her brother Phillip knew things. He knew the melodies so carefully, precisely plucked upon glistening webs by those daring diminutive courtiers who would play the wanton with the black widow spider and escape to tell the tale. He knew that his sister was in retreat from retreat, poorly prepared to take a plunge, prepared at best to spread her blanket on the brink and wait to see what would happen if nothing did.

Filomena read Flaubert while her brother looked her over, browsed through the card catalog of her memory, studied the position of what seemed to be her body as she sat in the rocker, carried away, disappearing into her book.

Phillip was a youngish Jungian, a carpenter and cultivator of magic mushrooms, a man of almost no words. But when the cabin grew dark he lit the fire and said, "Floating boat. Woman overboard."

Filomena as abandoned ship, as caravel or gondola, windjammer or ark, as vessel for fantasies and dreams, as gliding image, no one on board, no passengers complaining about the weather, about the food, about the long time it takes to get anywhere. "I could almost live with that," she told her brother.

"No sun," he countered.

"No seasickness," she replied.

"No wind."

"No fishy smell."

"No sex."

"Sans Freud."

"Sans sangfroid."

"Sans frustration."

"Sans fruit."

"Sans everything," Filomena conceded.

"It's your move," Phillip said. "Change happens."

Filomena was in the mood to take this as advice, so she unloosed her hair, ate honeydew, and dressed in sequined denim, not seeing until there was no turning back that the days had turned into weeks and her musing into mooning, a celestial kind of low howl longing that made her buy herself a long toboggan, exchange her set of Plato for a pair of platinum earrings, dream of Henry nearly bare on the beach in California, and sign up for mindwork with the local guru—one Doctor Stretcher, friend of Phillip's, a gray-haired downhill racer who each week greeted Filomena with a card trick and a randy sprawling of his legs atop his desk.

. . . "People call me Doc or Doctor Stretcher or Stretch or—"

"Enrico." Filomena had named him at their first meeting, had given a word to the Spanish moss of his eyebrows, the smoked catfish in his voice, the frank mediterranean ogle in his eyes that as Henry's devout companion she had ever observed and fathomed but had never yet experienced in quite this open ye rosebuds while ye may sort of way.

"Whatever you say, Red." Enrico wore white corduroy pants, a lemon-colored turtleneck, and heavy black ski boots. "Must be your bro detoured you in my direction. He calls me nada. Antiverbal dude, that one. Pick a card. Don't look at it."

Filomena took things seriously, pondered before she

picked. "So Phillip never speaks to you?"

"Which one?"

"You know my dead husband?"

"Theologistically speaking."

"Séances?"

"Mushrooms. One of your Phillips gives me the means, the other gives me the info. An immaterial witness." Enrico grinned. His body be-bopped a bit to some remembered tuneful toot.

"Witness to what?"

"You tell me."

"One's life has been full," said Filomena, meaning it and lying at the same time—old trick of Henry's.

"Full of beans, I hear. Replete with replications, simulations, substitutions, interpolations, intermezzos, full of prunes and pages, between the lines but not between the sheets. Slip that card into your pocket."

"My husband never complained."

"Neither did you."

"One has always something to give up."

"Could be I don't buy it."

Filomena wavered. "But there are precedents. Throughout history."

"There are pumps to be primed. Always have been, historically speaking. So let's get down to work. Time's a wastin'." Enrico swayed, he jived, he rocked.

"I'm not going to shrink," said Filomena.

But even on that first day she had named names, had spoken of Henry and of Cynthia, of the elegant simplicity of devotion to the dead. And she had made what she thought was an oblique reference to the self-portrait that had been hanging around unhung for years, unframed, now stored under her bed in her brother Phillip's cabin—a canvas the size of an oversize book in the center of which was a wide diagonal line, azure, almost black, an upward or a downward slope, stiff and curved. The self she had drawn resembled not at all the diagrams Enrico had displayed, dozens of them, pictures of selves as circles, as earths or globes, uncelestial bodies, some misshapen or incomplete, some surrounded or too small to see, some crashing into others, scrambled, geometrically obscure, dangerous figure-eights, slipshod halos, nearly every pair where pairs were concerned missing the symmetrical point that selves as circles are best as breasts, seeing as how—Enrico's words—they've got your built-in separation and your natural pliability.

"I'll stick with my line," said Filomena, swaying.

"Could be that's the point." Something in Enrico laughed—she could see it in his knees—as he shuffled his cards and took a gander out the window at the perfect pink circle of the see-ya'-later sun. "Curved and stiff," he said.

"More stiff."

"More curved."

Filomena fell into an ogle of her own, took off her shoes, and curled up, savoring suddenly the sound of *joyeuse*.

"Know what card you picked?"

Filomena guessed. "A deuce of hearts."

"Damn I'm good!" Enrico made confetti of his cards and poured champagne.

The work, as it were, had gone well.

*   *   *

. . . Phillip was for Filomena a novel experience, an embracer of evening skies and syrupy trees and older sisters, a man as tall as the regal Filomena, her confederate in point of view, her silent partner in the business of circumnavigation whose green mountain eyes told her one warm afternoon either "Don't worry" or "Let's eat" when Filomena nearing forty received a phone call.

The voice on the phone so startled her with its soft strumming of her post-Henry groin that Filomena had to sit for a while with her legs crossed, unable to think syntactically or make sense of the words that the voice on the phone seemed to have spoken: *vessel, vestige, investigation, something missing, lambent, adieu.*

It had something to do with Henry, that much she knew, with her connection, so to speak, the beans of which could have been spilled by only two persons: Cynthia, avenging earth-mother, alleged daughter, jealous lover of the master's implications, secret sewer in her dreams of the oft-bursting buttons on his vests; or the man she called Enrico, confidant and cha-cha coach, healer of minds by which he meant bodies. One of them (or someone else?) had let slip a word or had winked a wink that linked her to Henry, propounding sotto voce her complicity in a case of some sort. An investigation. Vessel. Adieu.

"I forgot I had a phone," said Phillip.

"You answered," said Filomena. "Did you recognize the voice?"

"Private dick," he told her. "On the side."

Phillip went into his room and returned with a mango-colored afghan that he wrapped around his sister's shoulders. "I made this," he said.

"What is he a private dick on the side *of?*"

Filomena waited while Phillip looked into this question. She dozed and dreamt of Henry circular, then took a walk and found a clearing from which she could see all the stars, and she had begun to give the constellations new names—Grecian Grapes, Banana Daiquiri, Concupiscence Unbound—when Phillip lay down next to her and said, "Beats me."

"I'm to be questioned tomorrow," Filomena told him.

"Wear your jumpsuit," her brother suggested.

. . . Filomena implicated, sheathed in her green silk jumpsuit, a womanly cucumber, found herself in Little Switzerland, in the tidy antique office of the private investigator, determined to defend her innocence, to practice subtle evasion, to disremember the voice on the phone.

But no can do!

Hunched like a raven though he was, this man who detected, this connoisseur of eau de toilette and bananas, this composer of heroic couplets and closet troubadour, this dainty man who in some sense questioned Filomena's whereabouts on the day and/or night that something of Henry's was discovered missing, was a man with whom she could not circumlocute.

"Cynthia." Filomena set the name in the detective's little lap.

"Forget her." He, too, had dressed for the occasion. He was wearing a tailor-made suit, lambswool, light brown, and a plum-colored tie. He took two iambic steps toward the seated Filomena. "Let us say you were with me."

"I was at the cabin. Reading." Filomena had told him these facts of the case already. "I am repeating myself," she said.

"Let us say that I was there with you. Turning the pages. Watching you repeat yourself."

"I was alone."

"Painting your toenails."

"I don't know your name."

"Preparing lobster bisque for lunch. Peeling peaches. Exposing my regrets."

"Are they large?"

"We did not sleep." His voice was tropical, it was an orchid, it was rum, it was filo dough. Filomena was moved.

"You don't look like an investigator," she told him. "You look like a man of letters."

"Love letters. Billet-doux. Messages passed beneath card tables in dimly lit drawing rooms. Notes slipped between your knees." His breath was butterflies, it was bath powder, it was feathers. Filomena felt round.

"Enrico," she said.

"Forget him. You may call me what you will." His breath was making a faint circle of dampness on the left shoulder of her jumpsuit.

Filomena was a grown woman. She put her hand on the lopsided rise of his back. "I know nothing of this disappearance," she said. "That I know of."

"I was there. Brushing your hair. Rubbing lotion on the small of your back. Investigating your innocence."

"Cynthia." Filomena tried once more.

"I am on the scent. We will make discoveries, you and I."

Filomena closed her eyes. "It will take some study," she whispered.

"The proper study of mankind," he seemed to say or softly sing, "is woman."

Filomena was coming unzipped, moving into the word-less world of pineapples and snowy owls.

She called him Matisse.

. . . It was not as though Filomena had never before found things surprising. For she had seen, when she was more or less seven, a watchful child named Helen, that her moonlike milky mother could spin herself a white cocoon and dream of flight forever. And she had not much later sat big-eyed and attentive while the semblance of her father, a shadow more distinct than the body it duplicated, became a grand and humorous magician whose best trick by far was to make her father disappear. And she had seen herself become a bookworm, a literal consumer of crisp pages whose appetite for aperture, for toothless meditative eating, cover to cover, astonished even the college librarian. And all those years with Henry—she had sizzled with half-suppressed surprise at the energy of her loyalty to a life worth living only as long as the figure of worth were kept dancing on a taut highwire unassisted, doing its pale pirouettes far above the popcorn-eating crowd. So she was not altogether amazed to find herself in her middling age in a maze of amorous play, dallying deliciously with Matisse, and learning to shake-rattle-and-roll with Enrico; nor did her otherwise animated eyebrows raise when she discovered that Enrico and Matisse were cousins of some sort, linked literarily by a Colorado balladeer whose rhymey songs had once been common in that long neck of the woods.

Nevertheless, the unflabbergasted Filomena was surprised beyond measure when her brother Phillip decided to give a dinner party.

"Call it a whim," Phillip told her as the two of them sipped hot wine before the fire.

"Is it a whim?"

"Call it a free-floating collective decision."

"What collective? I wasn't asked to vote."

"Call it arbitrary."

"I'm astounded."

"You're supposed to be."

"What do you have in mind?"

"Paella. Paper plates." No muscle, no crease, no nothing moved over Phillip's unfazable face, but those two or three who knew him would have called this one of his playful moments.

Filomena was one of those. "You're up to something," she said. "Something tricky, full fathom fiveish."

"A sea change."

"Who's invited?"

"Your suitors."

"I see an 'and' in your eyes."

"And Cynthia."

Filomena took this in. "You have no chairs," she said.

. . . Lavisher of the hottest spices on all that he ate, a talking eater, Enrico splashed interpretations of dreams at Phillip's extraterrestrial countenance while Matisse, smelling of Petrarchan sonnets and his host's paella, exchanged words about birds with the guest of honor, the saddened Cynthia, who sat cross-leggedly comfortable upon the highest and most inscrutable stack of books that Phillip had arranged around his workman's table in lieu of chairs, and who waited until late in the evening, after the flan had been eaten, after Filomena had poured the last of the wine into Phillip's jelly jars, to move her delicately ponderous presence from its perch and beckon Filomena to follow her.

They sat on the pillows in front of the fire. Cynthia fed the flames, peeling strips of wood from the dry logs, offering the strips to the fire as if they were pages, as if she were giving the fire its story.

"What I am about to tell you is that you are holding on. This is what I am now saying. You are clinging, as with pincers or barbecue tongs."

Thus spoke Cynthia. And in her voice she conveyed the sluggish reluctance of all the holders-on and clingers, the believers in locks of hair, the rememberers who are changed by change but who do not let go.

"I am saying to your face that you had him. Henry. No

one else could get at him for a decade. He was all Gloria's—''

"You kept trying."

"I am said to embody the words *steadfast, dutiful,* and *patient.* I am in agreement with this assessment. And yet. Nevertheless. Appearances to the contrary notwithstanding. I am capable of whimsy. I am admitting to a moment of temptation. To a few minutes, when Henry was all yours, of what they call gut-wrenching struggle. Yes, I considered throwing Henry over for a living author who goes by the name of Don. Probably a code name. But as you can see, my loyalty remained intact."

"I'm not Gloria anymore."

"I am telling you that I would never have given him up."

"I think he would have wanted me to live."

"To live. If you are speaking to me of the grief of choice, then I am replying yes. If you are having in mind what it means to know what you will never be, never do, never love, never have, then I am nodding my head in agreement."

"I mean—"

"To be stricken from behind, in the dark, with ever-to-be artistically avoided loss. This is what you mean, perhaps. I am saying perhaps because I am doubting." Cynthia, guardian of Henry's hesitations, retriever of lost words, waved one small hand toward the men at the table.

Filomena, fortified, nodded her head. "To live. I was thinking more along the lines of blueberries and babies and bad checks, that sort of thing."

"So it is true. You opt for nature. You choose what they call playing around. You turn your back on art. This has been heard of before. So why then do you cling? Why is it that you keep—perhaps in a picturesque portmanteau?—what should not be kept? What should never have been taken? Expunged, excised, extracted? I am pausing. Carried about—perhaps in a pillowcase?—as if, as relic, it would protect you from all future implications? I am saying that you have made your choice."

"You give me pause," said Filomena, momentarily discomposed by the magnificence of Cynthia's ardor, the way she rested her folded hands upon her full stomach, a simulacrum of the master. "You have suspected me all this while?"

"I believe that I have indicated to you that there was never a question of your complicity. Only of your power to so miraculously take and keep. I am lowering my voice. Yes, I initiated the investigation. I am confessing that I put the man you call Matisse on your tail. The mystery intrigued him. It seemed impossible. He claims to have made discoveries, but I have intuited that his professional tweed is misleading. His mind is on papaya juice and ankle bracelets. The other one, Enrico, says that he answered my urgent requests for information telepathically. He speaks of vibrations and Caribbean rhythms and pelvic telegrams. I am not listening to him. Body language I do not hear. And your brother, he invites, prepares paella, but takes no notice of my propinquity, of which he has ample clue. So it has been falling to me to unravel and retrieve and keep the whole affair under wraps. I am taking a breath."

Cynthia billowed, a bedazzling circumference, no gaps, no leaks.

"No one else knows?"

"I foresaw from the beginning general upheaval should this theft become known. There would be disbelief followed by unprofitable debate. Art everywhere would be threatened by this sorcery. I am imagining the insurance rates! What you did cannot be tolerated. It cannot happen!"

"It did happen. It was a gift, a remembrance."

"He is not the same."

"You are asking me to sacrifice."

"From *sacer,* sacred, and *facere,* to make. To make sacred."

"It is so little." But Filomena knew even as she said this that the word she as Gloria had taken from Henry's corpus had become something other than a lover's memento, something she might, as Filomena, extravagantly relinquish. She wondered if perhaps Cynthia were not, after all, Henry's daughter.

"It is everything. I say this without exaggeration. The corpus is disfigured. It is scarred. It is mutilated. (I am seeing the affect my words have on you.) It is as though he were missing the very eyebrow that had always been the most expressive of the two—the mediator, the reminder, the tattler, the tease, the ironist. End of list. You know that you must give it up."

Cynthia ballooned with the importance of her task, the preservation of the master's effects, his self-negating nu-

ances, those slippery swerves and curves around all that
to-do and to be. Henry, lambent.

"To make sacred," Cynthia repeated.

"To give up."

Filomena felt what was coming round the bend, an act of
acquiescence, a compliant completion of a circle of taking
and returning, a sacrifice she could more or less live with.
Yet as she rose, as she went to her room and opened the
closet, as she picked up the chest she had once called Hope
and then Treasure and then had forgotten (such were her
amores) to call anything, she filled herself with the memory
of Gloria's valediction, her adieu to the nothing that was
Henry's ghost by taking his palpable *something*, that moment when she chose her memento and Henry, silent, had
seemed to concede, to bequeath her his *something*, indeed
every ambivalent *something* he had ever roundaboutly ut-
tered on the page, so that the vague and artful word might
become by some consummate conjuring and clipping and
snipping something peculiarly hers—the exclusive property
of the once faithful but fruitless Gloria.

Filomena, no fool for love, had hung on just in case
change changed her again in such a way that she might need
something unpronounceable to fall back on, and for some
reason equally cautious she made sure that when she pro-
duced for Cynthia what Cynthia had come for, she held
back a little *something* for herself.

. . . Filomena got an inkling in *español* that night that just
about nothing was *imposible,* so she changed her name to

Consuela, bid her suitors passionate *hasta mañanas,* and invited the cerebral Cynthia for a ride on her toboggan down the mountain's steepest slope. Cynthia, sisterly—which is to say, triumphant—said "Sì, sì," though she took along for the ride and hug close to her chest the chest that was full of the heretofore lost word, knowing better than most what might happen to art if it's stored in the closet.

At the helm of her toboggan, Consuela drew through the bluish snow her self-imagining diagonal, the azure trace, but it was not long before some music, some sonata, some sweet cantaloupe rhythm began to guide the ride in a profound to and fro, a curve so quiet in the midnight snow that she could hear Cynthia's sleepy breathing, so still that she could feel her companion's small hands holding tight, the two of them bundled around something unspoken, a downy solidarity—which seemed to be what made the circle happen, what reversed the steady downward soar of the toboggan and drew it up the slope, up and around and down and up again in windy circle after circle, while the women in the dark in their different keys called out together, "Olé, Henry! Olé!"

The Golden Robe

I am not going to put on the lady's golden robe, even though it is the color of the body of my son. It is too soon. The robe is so heavy in my hands and it is also so light that I can roll it into a ball and hold it next to me under one arm. It rests against my hip. I know of no smoothness that is so smooth as the golden robe. But not one time until last night did I show to the lady how much I have wanted to touch the robe with both my hands and dream of somebody else's life.

The lady said I was to die for. She said it on the first day that I was brought to her and on many days after that. She made me speak long American sentences to the ladies who came to play cards in her living room. I do not know why she wanted to die for me.

Last night the lady said to me that the golden robe was to die for and that I knew why. But now it is resting against my hip and I am not dead.

I am remembering the first day, one year ago. The lady was so angry at the weather, which was very cold. It was even colder than it is today. Her red hands took away my coat and they took away my sweater and then they turned me in a circle so that she could see my whole self. The lady said she knew that I was different from other wetbacks. She said that she wanted me to love my room. She said that my room had been specially designed by a designer of rooms.

My room is behind the kitchen where there are blue and red and green tiles on the floor and on the walls and on the counters. The tiles in the lady's kitchen were made in my country. The lady owns many precious objects that were made so long ago by the Mayan people of my country. Many times company has come to her house to touch these objects and to stare at her view of the ocean and to eat the food that her caterers make.

My room is next to the room where I have washed and folded the lady's large white towels and where I have ironed her heavy white sheets and where only one time did I stroke my face and my neck with her undergarments, which have no color.

I do not need a mirror to know how I will look when I put on the golden robe. But there is a mirror in my bathroom. I am the only one who is supposed to use my bathroom, but many times I have found the lady's old son with his lips loose against the seat of my toilet, sick with drunkenness, so heavy and so soft when I have tried to lift him up and send him back to his own place that is on top of the lady's garage.

He comes to this house for his meals every day. He does not speak to the lady. He has knocked on the back door and on the front door this morning, but I have not let him in. One time he came to my room and cried for so long when I refused to suckle him.

Yesterday I became forty-eight years old. I said to the lady when she came into my room last night that I would never let my son's two golden daughters die in a room like this, but the lady did not answer.

I am not afraid. I am not afraid of the red eyes of the lady's old son. I am not afraid of the black water that surrounded the boat that brought me here. I am not afraid of the lady's hands. I am not afraid of this place that they call in my own language Marina del Rey.

The walls in my room are gray. The blinds are white. The drawers are white. The carpet is black. The bedspread is black and white and gray. On the wall beside the bed is a large painting of black and blue streaks. The towels in my bathroom are dark red like the color of the blood of my son.

I am remembering when the lady had so much company that she wanted her old son to stay in his place on top of her garage. But he would not go. He stayed with me in the kitchen and drank his liquor and talked. I did not look at him too many times. He is an albino man. He told me that he wears white clothes to hide it. I told him that he looks as if he were designed by the designer of my room. He laughed. His lips were pink and wet the whole time. The lady's caterers pretended that he was not there, even though he talked very much.

He asked me many questions about my son. What does he look like? Once he was golden. Once? Now he looks like you. Like me? Now he looks like death. Where does he live?

In a grave in the town of Concepción del Oro. He is dead? He could not swim fast enough. How old was he when he died? At the moment when the ocean filled his body he was very old. How old? Twenty-two. Was he married? He was. For how long? For three years that felt like three minutes. Children? Two. Boys? Girls. Where are they now? With the sisters at the Church of the Angels until I return. Was he brave? His hair was thick and wet. Was he strong? His dark eyes saw California. Was he handsome? He could not run fast enough. Can I stay with you when I take you back to your village? No. Can I stay with you? You cannot stay. Can I?

The lady's old son went to sleep on my bed. I sat on the white stool in my room and went to sleep two times. The second time I woke up and I knew that I must never put my brown hands around his white white throat and hold him tight against my hip. I woke up and I knew that his sickness was a sign. The lady's old son had vomited on the beautiful tiles on the kitchen floor many times.

I have cleaned all the tiles in the kitchen two times every week. One time every week I have polished the lady's silver. I do not like to polish the silver. In order to polish it I must look at it. I cannot look away. I always see my round brown face in the lady's shining silver trays. I do not see myself clearly, but I know that it is me.

I am remembering the silver vase that is so high and so wide that I must carry it with both my hands and still it is heavy. I had to see my face stretched out long and thin in the vase while I polished. I was not myself when I saw myself in that vase. Then I saw the lady's yellow hair and her long pink face in the vase next to mine. She smiled. In the vase the lady's smiling teeth were as long as the tiger's. I did not smile into the vase. But still we looked like long sisters. One pink, one brown, both silver. I could not make my eyes go away from those faces until the lady said to me that she wanted to wash my hair. I did not let her do that.

Now I will have to open the door and speak to the lady's old son. But first I must iron the wrinkles from the golden robe. The lady never put on the robe when it was wrinkled. She would always call someone who would come to her house and take the robe away. For a whole day the robe would be gone somewhere to be cleaned and ironed by strangers. Yesterday this happened. She would not let me do it. She did not worry when they took the robe away. I am the one who has always worried that they will lose it or steal it or forget to bring it back.

Last night I was asleep when the lady opened the door to my room and came in. She said for me to wake up and then she tried in my own language to wish me many more birthdays. She was wearing the golden robe. I was so happy that the robe was back with us. That was when I showed to her in my face what I had vowed not to show her.

She sat down on the end of my bed. She leaned her yellow hair against the gray wall and began to tell me her memories of many happy birthday parties. Her big teeth bit at her dry lips and made them bleed. Her long hands were red and so dry. They were holding a crystal goblet, like that of a priest. In the goblet there was milk mixed with liquor. The lady's yellow hair snapped from the static in the air. Strands of her snapping hair grabbed onto the gray wall where she was leaning. She ran one of her dry hands over the bedspread and laughed at the sparks that her hand made.

I got out of the bed. I put on my black sweater over my nightgown. I sat on the white stool in my room while the lady talked. The golden robe covered every part of her except her head and her hands. It also covered the bed and poured down onto the floor.

The lady drank from the goblet. She said that on her last birthday she gave herself the ruby ring that she wears on her right hand. She told me to look at the ring. She said that she might decide to give the ring to me. But I did not want to look at the ring because the lady's right hand was holding and rubbing her breasts. Her right hand with the ruby ring was moving the golden robe around and around her nipples. I did not want to look at the robe moving over and over the lady's breasts. It was my own breasts that the robe wanted most to touch.

I said that my year in her house was over. I said that her old son would take me back to my granddaughters. I said that I must go back. She could not make me stay. I said that I did not want the ruby ring. The lady pressed the golden robe between her legs.

I said that I did not know what to do.

The lady leaned toward me and I took the goblet from her. I drank some of the gray milk. She let the robe fall open. I did not want to see her soft pink body. I did not want to see her wrinkled stomach or her limp breasts that were swollen at the tips from rubbing.

The golden robe was everywhere.

The lady put some of it into her mouth. I knew that she wanted me to go into the robe with her. That is what she wanted me to do. Both of us inside the robe moving it over our breasts and between our legs in so smooth a circle many times. That is what she wanted us to do. She wanted us to love the robe. She took it out of her mouth and rubbed herself with the wet piece and said that I wanted it too, many times.

I told her that she must leave my room and that she must leave the golden robe with me. I do not know why I spoke to the lady as if I were the lady. I said that she will do as I say. I do not know why I said that. Then the lady stood up. Her yellow hair snapped and flew. She stood up so fast that the golden robe filled with air. The lady looked like a pink bat with golden wings that did not belong to it. The lady knew that is how she looked, but she did not care. I told her that she must leave the robe with me and that she must not move it over and over her breasts.

The lady laughed very loud. She brought the golden wings of the robe down and around me where I stood in front of the white stool in my room. When I did not let her kiss me on the mouth, she slapped me hard, two times, with the back of her hand. And then three more times. I slapped her back. I slapped the lady with the crystal goblet that was in my hand. I slapped it hard against her dry mouth and her pink ears. The rest of the gray milk splashed into her flying hair. The lady's face was bleeding. I hit her again. Then she fell down.

The golden robe was all over her. I could not see her. I did not want the blood from her face to soil the robe, so I removed it with both my hands because it is so heavy. I tried not to look at the lady curled up on the black carpet in my room.

Then she said that she wanted to give me something for my birthday. She said that she wanted to give me the golden robe.

That was all the lady said.

At home in my broken village I will put on the golden robe. Then I will stand atop the highest hill and look down upon the brown and yellow land that surrounds us. I will stare in the direction of the black and selfish ocean that gives me no peace. For many days I will supplicate the blank white sky while I feel the golden robe so smooth against my skin. The people of my village will gather at the bottom of the hill. They will gaze upon the golden robe for many days. And the ancient eyes that have lost their color will see that when I wear the golden robe I look like an Aztec princess. And the dead eyes that have watched the heavens every day and have seen always the same empty sky will believe that I look like an Angel of God. And the dark eyes that belong to the daughters of my son and have seen everything already will think that I look like the Statue of Liberty that stands somewhere in America.

A Love Story in One Act

"Believe me, mister, I say those words to you only because I'm supposed to tell you what didn't happen, right? So
here's the whole story: I had nothing to do with Tony Rambino going off in that ambulance and anyone who tells you
different is making up a fairy tale, don't ask me why. You
writing everything I say in your report? You got a nice face
on you, you know that? You must hear it all the time—"

"Actually, ma'am, I never—"

"And your face, it's saying to me, 'Lady, let's get this over
with because I don't have the whole night to spend with
you.' See? Look at the smile you got!"

"This isn't smiling."

"I don't have the whole night either, you know. I have to
pick up Silverio at eight-thirty—"

"Silverio?"

"Bellarocca."

"Silverio Bellarocca who sings in the opera?"

"You say his name good. But I was telling you that I have

to pick him up and then the two of us, we're going out for a late supper, somewhere not so dark you can't see the food on the plates. I don't know about *you,* but Silverio, he goes all day on a few pieces of fruit, a loaf of bread, some cheese, some salami—that's all. So at night, he *eats*! Two, three plates of pasta, a dish of meatballs, greens, *madon*! by the armful, and—"

"And cannoli?"

"Silverio doesn't touch them and he doesn't know one thing about this mix-up over Rambino, believe me. He was already at the rehearsal when it happened. What did you say your name was again?"

"Officer Corelli, ma'am."

"You heard of Franco Corelli? He's been on my shit-list lately. Don't tell me you're related to *that* one!"

"No connection."

"That's good. I could tell. I won't give you all the details of how he ended up on my list, so don't worry. Where was I? Those words I didn't say—"

"The ones you said to me—"

"Maybe some words like them did go through my mind, very fast, after what that floozie said about Silverio, and then (you putting this down? I'm a lefty, too, you know)—and then right after that I said to myself, in private, 'The next man or woman who says to me Silverio Bellarocca is too fat to play the lover, that person will wish they were—"

"Dead?!"

"I didn't mean anything to happen, Mr. Corelli! A disappearing idea, that's all it was. I didn't even whisper it. Are you Luisa's youngest son by any chance?"

"No—"

"Luisa and me, we both got married right after we graduated, seventeen years old, like there was nothing to it. And then one day I look up from the sink in my kitchen and my husband, so-called, is going over to Korea for a war, and out of the blue sky a couple years later I get a letter from him saying he's gonna stay there forever, right in Korea. . . . He's got some children over there now, I heard. But that Luisa! She's a whole other story! Still married to Ricky Corelli, and I don't need to tell you about *that* one! I bet he's made this chair warm plenty of times—"

"Plenty. Same chair."

"You got a comfortable room here. The last time I saw Luisa we were both getting our hair cut over at Tootsie's. And Luisa, she was giving me the frozen shoulder because me and Silverio are an item—"

"Ma'am, hey. We need to get on with this report."

"Why don't you call me Miss de Palma? It's right there on that piece of paper the other policeman gave you who needs a shave. See? They put my age down there, too. You mind calling an old woman 'Miss,' or what?"

"I don't see any old women around here."

"Ooh, what manners on this one! All right, Mr. Corelli, like I said, I will answer all your questions."

"Like what did the quote floozie unquote say to you that made you so angry?"

"First you have to know I wasn't *so* angry. That Teresa, who runs things over at the Florentine Bakery, she can't tell shit from shinola. Believe me, I'm never going there again for my coffee-an'. When hell is an iceberg is when I'll go.

For thirty years I've been going there faithful for my coffee-and-cake—"

"Coffee-and-cannoli?"

"There you go with the cannoli again, you *diavolo*! Once in the blue moon I'll have one, that's all. What I'm trying to tell you is Teresa blames *me*—"

"For what happened to Tony Rambino—"

"Do this for me, okay? In your report, write down for me that Rose de Palma is going to Caruso's Bakery from now on."

"In the report?"

"To make it in writing."

" '. . . from now on.' "

"That's good. I know I have a little temper on me sometimes, Mr. Corelli. But I held back when things got started over at the Florentine, just like I held back when that bag who calls herself Ronnie made those insults to my face. Excuse my French. The shoes fit, so what are you gonna do?"

"This Ronnie . . . she's the skinny one who gave her name as Veronica de Spirito Santo?"

"She can call herself Jesus-Mary-and-Joseph and she'd still be a bag, believe me. You think this is a laughing matter, Mr. Corelli? Who knows. Now here's what happened. I'm downtown. I'm putting up the announcements."

"Announcements?"

"For the *Tosca*! Next month it starts. They look real good—a pale blue background with fancy lettering all in black. Thirty-two inches by thirty-six. A good size, yes? I'll bring you one for your room here, special. Tomorrow morning. You have your tickets for the *Tosca* yet? I've got some right here in my pocketbook—"

"Miss de Palma. Do you know why we're here, you and me?"

"For me to give you my side of the story."

"And we keep going off the track."

"We're not going anywhere, Mr. Corelli, believe me. You'll see. You've got to keep your pants on so I can give you all the facts, like they do it on the TV—"

"We're talking facts here?"

"Look: I was bothering nobody. I was down at the shoe store taping one of the posters to the window that faces Genesee Street. And from out of nowhere this Ronnie walks by and starts laughing, loud, right in my face—"

"Laughing at what?"

"At the *announcement,* Mr. Corelli!"

"Of course!"

"And so I say to her in a nice voice, 'What are you laughing at, you piece of dirt?' and she says back to me in that high voice of hers that gives me a headache from here to here, she says, 'At that fat boyfriend of yours who thinks he's some kind of opera hero! Hah!' she says to me. *'Buffone enorme!'* she says. . . . Mr. Corelli, she's screeching out these things, and more, too, about how Silverio's gonna look when he's made up like Cavaradossi in the painter's smock he wears in the first act. 'A circus tent!' she hollers. 'People laugh behind his back!' she tells me. And everyone on the street there can hear her words that are like a piercing arrow in my stomach, right here, low, you know what I mean?"

"A piercing arrow."

"That's right. But no matter what Ronnie says to me, I don't start anything. I hold back. I just say to her, 'What can a bag like you know about opera and who can look like what?' And that's when she says to me, 'Oh, *everybody* knows that a beautiful woman like Floria Tosca would *never* throw herself away on some fat painter who can't even see his own *cogliones* without looking in the mirror!' That's what she said. You married, Mr. Corelli? You got a nice handwriting for a man—"

"Miss de Palma. I'm sorry about what that woman said. But what I need to know is—"

"She's a bag. That's all. She don't know nothing about nothing. So are you married, or what?"

"I see somebody now and then. You know."

"Your girlfriend, she's slim?"

"You could call her slim, I guess."

"You *guess*?! What kind of man doesn't know the size of his girlfriend? Never mind—maybe it's good you don't know the difference. You're not in love with her weight, right? You like the opera, Mr. Corelli?"

"I love the opera, Miss de Palma, but—"

"And your girlfriend? She does too?"

"She's a music major. Over at the city college. A singer, in fact. A mezzo—"

"So you see? You have a girlfriend who knows just what I'm talking about. If you want to sing like a god you have to eat like an animal. What's her name?"

"Adrianna. I wouldn't call her my girlfriend. Okay. Enough. We need to get back to—"

"My father's sister, my aunt had that name. Adrianna. But then one time she went to Cleveland and—"

"Miss de Palma, when you look at me what do you see? A patient guy, right? A policeman who has in front of him on this table a report form that is still almost blank except for the parts that don't—"

"Like I've been trying to tell you, I just walked away from that bag. I knew I better go someplace and have a cup of coffee and a piece of cake. To calm down. I made sure the announcement was taped good to the window, then I walked away with that feeling in my stomach I told you, like I was stabbed—"

"And then what?"

"I got on the bus. I put my twenty-five cents in that thing on the bus. I sat down near the bus driver. His name is Joe something or other. I rode over to Bleecker Street. I kept my face to myself. I walked the couple of blocks over to the Florentine. . . . Is this how I have to tell it? Just I did this and then this?"

"That's fine, ma'am."

"That's fine, ma'am, he says to me! Like I was a stranger! *Pe'la miseria!* I'll tell you one thing, Mr. Corelli—"

"Tell me."

"This whole business about Silverio and those insults and your girlfriend who sings in the college, the whole thing has you nervous—"

"*What* whole thing?"

"You have a record player at home? All you young people have them, right? Okay. I want you to do me this favor with your record player. I want you to listen to some of those

skinny opera singers. Like little Tito Schipa. He's one. I'll
bring you a record of his—"

"I have one, Miss de Palma. I'll listen to it."

"I'm not trying to tell you that Mr. Schipa has nothing for
a voice. He gets each note perfect, no? But I want you to
ask yourself this question when you listen tonight to your
record: Has Mr. Tito Schipa ever had the hots for anybody?
Ask Adrianna. Ask all your friends. I think they will say he's
like a beautiful little flute, no, a piccolo, a pretty sound, but
no body—"

"No *passione*."

"You hit him on the head."

"But let's face it, Miss de Palma. Schipa doesn't have
anything to do with why—"

"Maria Callas is another one. When she got skinny like a
Hollywood movie star, her voice went down the toilet, all
the way—"

"*And?*"

"And I bet Adrianna is glad she has a nice boyfriend like
you who reminds me of—"

"And because I'm nice, you're gonna tell me what happened, right?"

"For you. That's what I'm doing. But you already know
the main part about that phony baloney music critic Tony
Rambino. Maybe he deserved what he got, I won't be the
judge of it. But the jealousy of that cockaroach, it's a terrible
thing to see with your eyes!"

"So Rambino, he's jealous of, uh, your, you know, your
relationship with Mr. Bellarocca, is that it?"

"The way you say 'uh your relationship,' you make it

sound like we got something to hide. I'm what they call his mistress, that's all. You can write that down, go ahead—''

"It fits into the story?"

"Everything fits, Mr. Corelli."

"What about Rambino? I still don't follow—"

"He's in love with himself! That's how he fits and that's why he hates Silverio and puts lies about him in the papers—"

"That's all there is to it?"

"When I was young, Mr. Corelli, we didn't know one thing about what goes on between a man and a woman. We went by how it looked in the movies: a moon, a piece of music, a kiss, marriage—always between a young man and a young woman who had dancing lessons when they were children and haircuts just so, slim figures, new clothes, and they always held each other when they kissed like this—''

"Like this?"

"That's right. By the shoulders. Then they would peck each other, like birds with no lips. It took me a long time before I knew (you can let go now, Mr. Corelli), before I knew they were kissing that way so their bodily parts wouldn't start getting ideas. What do you think one of those movie women would say if someone came up to her in front of the shoe store and said, 'I don't think your husband can see his own *cogliones* he's so fat'? She'd say, 'What are *cogliones*?' That's how they are, those people—"

"But you, Miss de Palma, you'd say something like—"

"I didn't mean to give you the idea that Rambino has the hots for me. I won't say he never thought of it. But he knows what I think about the crapola he puts in the papers, like

when he wrote down that any man or woman who thinks
Silverio is outta this world has some kinda disease he called
the 'fat fetish.' Or when he wrote down that nobody can
take Bellarocca *seriously* as a lover. What a miserable bastard he is, believe me.''

''I do.''

''He doesn't know a lover from a hole in the dirt. But I'll
tell you this: Silverio knows who he is.''

''This doesn't surprise me.''

''And being a lover is number one with him. Along with
his music, which is also number one. And that's why people
can't help, you know—how can I say it?—they can't help
getting *swept over* toward Silverio, the way the leaves always go toward the gravity—''

''It's nature.''

''You read my mind, Mr. Corelli.''

''I've heard him sing.''

''He's a huge man.''

''I know.''

''And when he's singing, it's like he's touching you over
here and over here, around your face and neck and down
your back, like you were a beautiful piece of fruit, and he's
lifting you, Mr. Corelli, carrying you, like in a dance. And
you get the goose bumps in every spot. And you think: How
alive these arms are! You never think: These are fat arms.
Even before I was with him the first time, in bed, I could
imagine how it would be to make love with him. . . . You
can tell from his singing that he would caress each part of
you as if it was the first time and the last time. He would hold
you the way he holds some notes, like he can't believe the

beauty, so he holds on as long as he can, and even he's surprised, you know, it's so good. That's how I imagined it would be with him—"

"And you were right—"

"Yes."

"Lifting."

"Yes."

"I'm losing track."

"You look like you're on vacation in Florida all of a sudden."

"Where was I?"

"I don't know, Mr. Corelli."

"The events that went on . . . at the Florentine."

"These *are* the events."

"The first time making love with Silverio Bellarocca? Holding onto the fruit?"

"It's all part of the story."

"I shoulda seen that."

"You have to trust me."

"I trust you. You have my trust. But let's say there was a third party in here in with us, somebody listening, anybody. If you ask me, the third party would tell us we haven't got to the heart of the matter—"

"But *we* know the heart when we see it, yes?"

"You don't want to let the third party in on it?"

"It is no secret. Tony Rambino is a man gone crazy with love for himself. That's all there is to it. Take the way Silverio sings *'E Lucevan le Stelle,'* that aria from *Tosca,* in the last act. You know it?"

"Sure. *'E lucevan le stelle.'* . . ."

"That's the tune. I've heard it a million times sung by the famous tenors with the big records—"

"Me, too, Miss de Palma."

"So you know the story."

"Frontwards and backwards."

"There's Mr. Cavaradossi, sitting around in the dungeon, all alone, waiting to be executed—"

"Remembering what it was like to make love with Tosca, all those *'languide carezze.'* . . ."

"Yes. But most of those other tenors, they sing the words like—how can I explain it?—it's like they're still alive, you know, but their whole groin area, all through here, it's already executed—"

"Finito!"

"Silverio, when he sings it, everything's still living! And you know that if Tosca walked in, he would make love with her again, right in that dungeon. Those others, they're so busy crying over the spilled milk of life, if Tosca walked into the room—"

"They couldn't do nothing."

"You take the words from my mouth! Look, Mr. Corelli. Look at this here, how this loose skin along my arms, underneath, how it jiggles when I wave good-bye to somebody. And I fill out these stretch pants pretty good, too, don't I? . . . What? These stretch pants make you a little *pazzo,* Mr. Corelli? They make you hum?"

". . . just trying to remember the words. . . . You go on, I'm listening. . . ."

"Well, I was saying that Silverio—"

" *'Ma nel ritrar costei'*—"

"Silverio says it's me he's singing about—"

" 'Il mio solo pensiero'—"

"When he sings that aria—"

" 'Ah! mio solo pensier sei tu!'—"

"He imagines *me* for his Floria Tosca—"

" 'Tosca, sei tu!' "

"Bravo, Mr. Corelli! You fill me up with surprise! Why didn't you say all this time you were a singer?"

"I'm not, Miss de Palma. I don't know what got into me."

"It was Silverio."

"What?"

"Come with me to the rehearsal at St. Anthony's tonight. I will have you meet *don* Sardo and you could—"

"Hey, no, I can't do that. I like to sing, sure, but not for real. Besides, I've got a full-time job here."

"Lots of the singers work at jobs during the day."

"What I do is, I'm a policeman."

"I remember that part."

"So you know the hours, they aren't so regular, and sometimes the people you have to question are—"

"I forgot to tell you there was somebody else over there, at the Florentine—"

"Somebody else?"

"I never knew a singing policeman like you before."

"Rose, you wanna tell me about this somebody else?"

"Which one?"

"I called you Rose."

"You got a rule against a first-name basis?"

"A rule? No, no rule—"

"So maybe I could call you—?"

"Aurelio. Named after my grandfather on my mother's side. But everyone around here calls me Larry—"

"You're giving me a look, Aurelio."

"I am?"

"Like you got ideas cooking in the oven and part of you's watching them rise."

". . . . You're gonna tell me what happened, Rose. I can feel it."

"You know, maybe you're not cut out for this police business. Like my brother Julio. He used to be a policeman. Now he makes bread for the tourists down in Cooperstown."

"My job's all right. Usually I'm real good at it."

"Maybe sometime you'll want another line of work, who can tell? Maybe my brother Julio could help you out. Can you knead?"

"As in I need you, you need me?"

"Knead the dough, you chooch! Like this here."

"I could do that, yeah."

"You ever been to that museum they have for baseball things down in Cooperstown?"

"You don't want to tell me the story, do you?"

"Look at us here: like two peas in the pod getting to know each other."

"Rose, if I could be you, I would. . . . But we have to finish it."

"We do?"

"My job, you know? That's why we're here."

"The rest of the story—"

"Yes. As a personal favor."

"Okay, Aurelio."

"Okay."

"Here it is."

"Go."

"I got to the Florentine and I saw my girlfriend Ang and sat down with her—"

"Got it."

"Ang just had a permanent done to her hair, you could smell the chemicals all over the place, but she's my best friend, so I didn't notice it. We had some sponge cake, plain, no icing or fruit or nothing. My stomach still didn't feel too good—"

"Keep going, Rose—"

"Me and Ang drank some black coffee. Two cups. She says to me, 'Rose, don't let these Ronnies get your blood pressures going up.' And I say back to her, 'Ang, the way they talk, it's a terrible thing in this world—' "

"Good. Don't stop."

"After we finished talking about Ronnie we started in on Ang's cousins down in Florida. We ate another piece of cake. We were minding our own business. All the trouble started when those others—"

"Which others? When they what?"

"This isn't coming out so good, Aurelio."

"What do you mean? What do you mean not coming out?"

"I don't know. It doesn't sound good to me."

"It sounds great!"

"It needs something."

"It needs nothing, Rose, believe me—"

"If I only had a voice like yours—"

"Like mine?"

"Then maybe I could tell it with more . . . something, more range, up and down."

"The way you tell it, it's beautiful."

"You think so? I don't think so."

"*Beautiful!* I know what I'm talking about. So what happened next?"

"When those others—?"

"Yeah, who? Ronnie? Rambino?"

"And that other one—"

"They all came in together, or what?"

"If you were telling it, how would they come in?"

"If I—? Hold it! Hold on, Rose—!"

"What a good idea, Aurelio!"

"Which idea?"

"*You* tell it!"

"*Me?*"

"Why not?"

"I could give you twenty reasons at least!"

"But you don't want to, believe me."

"Rose, look—"

"You could pretend—"

"*Madonna mia, aiudame!*"

"Well?"

". . . . You wanna sit in my chair?"

"This one's got my shape in it by now—"

"You know when I was a kid we had this chair in the parlor my grandmother brought with her from the old country, don't ask me how—a rocker covered over in this tapestry material that my sister Anna's got now and she—''

"Mr. Corelli?"

"Yes?"

"The story—"

"Right."

"I'm ready."

"Okay. Let's see. . . . We all know you're not the kind of woman who goes around saying the words *go shit on your*—''

"God forbid!"

"Right. But you had this feeling like an arrow in your stomach—''

"Everybody knows this part already—''

"You had this piercing feeling and you were thinking about it, you were thinking about the insults to Silverio, you were thinking about how they laugh behind his back, you were thinking all this just before you walked away from Ronnie—''

"I was holding back—''

"*Exactly!* You were thinking and holding back at the same time! And while you were thinking and holding back, what happened was, those words, Rose, without you knowing, they somehow slipped right out of your mouth—''

"*Jesu!*"

"You would never say them. But you did—''

"I did?"

"And so Ronnie caught the next bus over to Bleecker Street and showed up at the Florentine acting like she didn't do anything and telling everybody in sight that you said she should go shit on her mother's—''

"The lowest bag is what she is!"

"And then the woman named Teresa, the redhead, your former friend who manages the Florentine, right? She gets into the act and sides with Ronnie—"

"A traitor, that Teresa!"

"She sides with Ronnie and says to you, 'Rose de Palma, you better take your dirty mouth someplace else.' And then, yeah, you say something back to Teresa like, 'Why do you believe the one with a butcher's knife for a face?' That's what you say, Rose, with your head up, proud, like this—"

"Like this—?"

"A little higher. Good. That's it. Where was I? You're giving Teresa a piece of your mind, telling her you're gonna go to Caruso's from now on—"

"It's in writing in our report, I should tell her—"

"And then, at that moment, the way I see it, Tony Rambino comes into the Florentine! He's wearing a light blue silk suit and a hat pushed over to the side, miserable bastard style, and he's smoking one of those crooked little cigars, you know the kind, and behind him, following in his little footsteps, there's this friend of his, Cliff—"

"Cliff?"

"Yeah, the somebody else! Friend of Rambino's, big guy, makes Tony look like a puppet. So what do they do? They start egging Ronnie on about this beef she has with you and before you know it she's telling them what she said about Silverio not seeing his own *cogliones* without looking in the mirror! The mouth on that bag! I'm telling you—"

"You're telling *me*?"

"The three of them are laughing, Rambino's howling like

a dog. You and Ang are trying to mind your own business. But what happens is, this Cliff guy, he comes over to your table, he's standing there, laughing, and then he says to you, 'Hey, Silverio's not the only one!' "

"He talks in that voice?"

"In the meantime, we got Ronnie and Rambino still standing over at the counter, we got them waiting for their coffee and cannoli, not paying too much attention to their friend Cliff, so they don't hear so good when you ask him, 'Silverio's not the only one *what*?' And they don't hear so good when Cliff answers, 'Who can't see them things without a mirror!'—"

"Who does he think he is to talk to me that way?!"

"That's just what you're saying to yourself when you get up, like you're getting ready to leave. And then Cliff, he comes over to you, close, like he's gonna whisper something in your ear. But you step back, Rose—"

"That's good. That's good I did that."

"You step back and you say to Cliff, 'What are you talking about, you *cafone*?' And he says to you, 'I'm talking about *Tony*!' "

"*Rambino?!*"

" '*Rambino?!*' you say, Rose, loud enough so the ones over at the counter can hear it real good. And you say, 'But, Cliff—' "

"I know his name?"

"Yeah. You ask him, 'But, Cliff, how can it be? Rambino, he's so *thin*?!' "

"Like a snake—"

" 'He's thin as a snake!' you say to Cliff. And Cliff says

back to you, laughing, forgetting Rambino's right behind him, he says, 'You figure it out!' And the next thing you know, Rose, Rambino starts to *strangle*!''

"*Strangle?*"

"And Ronnie screams out she saw Rambino jam a cannoli down his throat when he heard what his good friend Cliff said about his private parts in public!''

"Ronnie said that?"

"Who knows? But let's say she did, let's say she goes to the other shops up and down Bleecker Street, let's say she tells everybody she runs into that Tony Rambino, Utica's big-deal music critic, is over at the Florentine trying to kill himself on a cannoli!''

"Kill himself?! On a cannoli?!"

"Maybe that's how it looked! Why not? So there's Rambino choking by the counter, and over here's Teresa saying it was all your fault, and your friend Ang is standing next to you saying it was all Ronnie's fault, and Cliff, he's hitting Rambino on the back, saying it was all the fault of the cannoli, right? Too big around for Tony's mouth! Everybody's talking at once. Somebody calls the ambulance, somebody calls the police, everybody's waiting for me to arrive on the scene. . . . I arrive. I park my car. I step out, like this. I walk into the crowd. People from all over have something to say to me about it—this and that, how hard, how soft, who's right, who's wrong. They're all crowding around me—''

"I couldn't get a word into it—"

"There's maybe a hundred people all bunched up around me outside the Florentine!''

"A hundred, Aurelio?"

"Let's say seventy-five, at least, believe me, and all of them are waiting to get a look at Rambino and his cannoli when he comes out on the stretcher, and all of them are watching me ask questions, take down names, conduct official police business, you know what I mean? Then somebody brings me a cup of coffee—"

"That was me."

"It was? I mean, there were so many people crowded around me—"

"Aurelio—"

"I know it was you, Rose."

"So then what happens?"

"Then I come back here and you show up to give me your side of the story for the report."

"That's the ending?"

"You could tell me in your own words what went on—"

"I like the way you tell it. It's better."

"Better than *what*?"

"Aurelio. . . . Aurelio Corelli. Your grandfather! *His* name was Aurelio Corelli!"

"Yeah, remember? I told you—"

"He sold tickets at the train station all his life. He was the best fortune-teller I ever knew! Whenever I had to go someplace on the train, I always went to his booth. He read the fortunes off the tickets you bought. You got your looks from him, you know that? I was a girl of no woman's age when he told me I would love a singing man who would rise like the sun."

"What do you say we take a walk over there?"

"To the train station?"

"It's only a couple of blocks. We'll get some coffee. And a piece of cake. To calm down. Then you can go meet Signor Silverio Bellarocca, after we talk—"

"Would you give me a hand with this coat?"

"Sure. I was saying that maybe over coffee you'll tell me—"

"Maybe. . . . Ah, he offers me his arm! My dear Aurelio. Now, where were we? Swept over, yes?"

"Like leaves, Rose, yeah."

A NOTE ABOUT THE AUTHOR

Melissa Lentricchia, who is from Riverside, California, teaches literature and creative writing at Duke University, where two of her plays have premiered. She is the managing editor of the *South Atlantic Quarterly*. Her stories have appeared in such journals as *Antaeus*, the *Kenyon Review*, and *Fiction International*.